what if i got down on my knees?

a series of romantic misadventures and entanglements

tony rauch

WHISTLING SHADE
PRESS

1495 Midway Pkwy St. Paul   MN   55108
www.whistlingshade.com

First Edition, First Printing
April 2015

Stories in this collection have appeared, in slightly different versions,
in the following publications:
"in the dust"—*Revolver* (Minneapolis, MN)
"lets get sad", "in the sun"—*Daily Love*
"congratulations"—*New Dead Families*
"hooray for all the children"—*Split Quarterly*
"silhouette"- *Smashed Cat*
"the idiot's guide to morons"—*Rivet Journal*
"how you felt when I disappointed you"—*Blink Again* (anthology, Spout Press)
"althea (moonlight)"—*Whistling Shade*
"big baby"—*New Dead Families*

ISBN 978-0-9829335-5-8

Cover design by Tony Rauch and Joel Van Valin
Book Design by Joel Van Valin

Printed in the United States of America

Other story collections by Tony Rauch:

I'm right here (Spout Press)
Laredo (Eraserhead Press)
eyeballs growing all over me ... again (Eraserhead Press)

The author would like to thank the following for their assistance, support, and/or encouragement in assembling this collection: Margaret Rauch, Jeremy Maddox, Spout Press, Eraserhead Press, Whistling Shade Press, Joel Van Valin, Sten Johnson, Iris Key, Michael Gause, Dylan Garcia-Wahl, Deborah Steinberg. Thanks for listening.

She wasn't doing a thing that I could see, except standing there leaning on the balcony railing, holding the universe together.

- J. D. Salinger, *A Girl I Knew*

The curves of your lips rewrite history.

- Oscar Wilde, *The Picture of Dorian Gray*

It frightened him to think what must have gone to the making of her eyes.

- Edith Wharton, *The Age of Innocence*

In Maple Rock there was no "town drunk."
We had "the sober guy."

- Michael 'Spam' Hall

Whether you succeed or not is irrelevant, there is no such thing. Making your unknown known is the important thing ... and keeping the unknown always beyond you.

- Georgia O'Keeffe

contents

shiny things

for Lee Russo

—rock on

please don't go

in the dust

Me and Elmer had to get out of town.

We barely made it to the rail yard for the 4:35. We had to crawl through one hundred feet of the driest underbrush and burs and thickets and sharpies. We had to race for the train as it tugged away from us.

The cops had been out looking for us all day. We had been stealing dogs again. I'm not really sure why we stole dogs. It was just something to do. Something to lull away steamy summer days like this.

Me and Elmer would herd the dogs together in a ditch and get 'em all riled up. We weren't mean to 'em 'r anything, we just liked herdin' 'em an' runnin' 'em through the cool rivers of shade, each a great sailing ship of its own, sailing to exotic lands through the dusty back alleys and gardens and yards of town—a hundred dogs in a great dog stampede, a great stream of smelly fur flowing through yards and gas stations and the supermarket. If you've ever seen a hundred dogs racing through an alley, you can attest to what a moving and inspiring event it can be—if done properly. The sight was so winsome, so captivating, that's why I couldn't understand why the authorities found it to be so disruptive. So what if we raced a stream of dogs through the supermarket, the church, city hall. This was our art, and we were providing them a moment of beauty, a respite from their monotonous, bland lives.

The train clickety-clacked us out of town as a couple of older, out-of-shape cops tried to catch up, waving their batons to bust our heads clean open. And who could blame 'em, really? I mean, we'd taken a couple of their dogs an' gone an' gotten 'em all worked up. Dang, if I had dogs an' some bored, unemployed guys with nothin' ta do took 'em an' ran 'em 'round town, adding dog after dog to their temporary collection... Well, dang, I don't know what I'd do. I mean, that's the type a thing that could really set a guy off.

Elmer whistled as we gently swayed to and fro, back and forth, rocking side-to-side like the wind blowing waves in the amber fields of rolling grain, the grain our ocean, the boxcar our great sailing ship.

I liked Elmer. He'd talk for hours about how each of the great poets had met their end. He knew all the little details, many of which I bet not even the family members were aware of. Many of these circumstances were quite embarrassing, or perhaps they were all just made up.

"Take us to the end of the world!!" I called, hanging out the boxcar's door, the wind blowing in my hair and on my face like freedom, until Elmer pushed me out with his foot and the cops caught up as I tumbled in the dust.

They broke my arm with an old two-by-four that was layin' there in the ditch. Said I was resistin'.

The cell was empty. Just a little sink and a cracked and chipped jumble of porcelain that passed for a toilet. Least they had indoor plumbin'.

They only fed me dog food. Seemed fitting.

I spent my days on the cold cement floor, daydreaming of the day of the great dog flood—me leadin' a thousand, no wait, *three* thousand assorted dogs, all types and sizes—all breeds racin' through town to Elmer's grave. A thundering stream of wild beasts and me, gigglin' and runnin' in victory—finally pullin' off the greatest dog run in recorded history. We'd dig ol' Elmer up an' scatter his bones throughout the dusty town, throughout time.

I picture Elmer now, sittin' at the end of the world, maybe catchin' a nap in the shade beside a gentle little creek. Maybe he'd even have a dog beside him in the grass there. Or maybe I was the one at the end of the world, sittin' here while he was in some boxcar gently rocking side-to-side, on his way back to the world, back to excitement.

My excruciating loneliness is broken periodically by a random dog barking in the distance. This is the only thing that keeps me going now, that gives me hope. The only thing that gives me faith—as if each dog were calling out to me, looking for me in the weeds and tall grass, in the dust of the alleys. All this time in here, I hope they're out there lookin' for me.

let's get sad

It's finally a rainy day. So a bunch of us hit the basement. It's totally gloomy out, oppressively gray and bleak, the perfect setting for getting sad.

"Finally, a crummy day," someone beams.

"Yeah, maybe this'll finally impress the girls," Johnny D nods to himself.

"Nothin' else seems to be workin'," Kenny shrugs.

So we set about getting sad. We watch the movies *Brian's Song* and *Bambi*, take turns reading the obituaries out loud (the illnesses, the war, the accidents, the randomness, the unfairness, the instability, the falling, the veering, the wobbling, the looseness, the waste of it all), and listen to really sad music (principally The Smiths, some glum classical [Samuel Barber's "Adagio for Strings" and "Angus Dei"—the string and vocal versions], samplings of Lou Reed's *Berlin* album, and a smattering of alternative college stuff such as The Wild Colonial's "Spark" and The Violent Femme's "Good Feeling", and some classics like Sinatra's "September of My Years" and "Send in the Clowns" [the version by Judy Collins]).

"Are you really sad yet?" I ask Benny as I stare blankly into my desolate future.

"Yeah," he mumbles.

"Just sad? Or *really* sad?" I inquire, still staring, as if I simply can't bring myself to move.

"I wanna freakin' off myself, man," he whines.

"Good. Good," I nod, "I think you're there then. I think you're ready."

"I wanna freakin' end it all, man," he turns away to bury his face into the couch, "Why did Bambi's mom have to die, man? Why? ... What's the point of it all?"

"I think my heart has died," Kenny gasps, "Man, I ... I really think I went too far on this one, I mean, I'm in way too deep here..."

"Great, man," I moan encouragement, "Keep goin' deeper."

"My heart's dead," Kenny squeals, slithering on the rug, turning over, writhing in pain, "It's gone ... it's gone," he wheezes and gasps, "soon it will all be over ... soon."

"Good," I nod, "Go with that." Then I look over to Pharaoh, "How's it workin' for ya?"

"Why?" he quivers, sitting on an apple crate, his head in his hands, "Why?" he shudders, "Why?"

"I think we're ready," I utter.

Someone groans.

"We should've had a person monitoring our progress," I sigh, "I think we've gone too deep ... overplayed our hands." I try to get up, but can't. I try again, succeeding to stand this time. "Come on. Let's go," I whisper, "We're ready... Let's get to it," I wave to the door, but everyone's scattered like limp blankets.

"Yeah," Pharaoh gulps, rising sloppily off the floor, "This is it."

"This is our big chance," I wheeze, "To finally impress those cool, sensitive, arty college chicks. Not the usual impressionable morons, but the thoughtful, literate types."

"Nothin' else has worked, so maybe this'll do," Pharaoh gulps sadly, rubbing his eyes.

"Yeah," someone whispers sadly, "Now we're 'deep'."

Kenny slowly rolls over, sits up, rises to his feet, collects himself, stares down, "Maybe this will help," he nods.

"Oh, man," someone on the floor groans, "Just leave me be..."

We step over and pull him up. It's Johnny D. He flops down as he goes limp. We lug him to the door and out the basement steps. He wiggles in our arms, trying to get free.

"Yeah, let's hit that tapestry exhibit by those refugees," Kenny mumbles vacantly, "I'm sure they'll be some bespectacled sensitive types there..."

"Let's show 'em how sensitive and in touch with our inner emotions we are..." I moan as we climb the steps, "There's supposed to be a poetry reading on death and loss afterwards."

"We can only hope," Johnny D groans as we lug him out into the gloom.

when Jesus and I played football

It was from 1967 to 1969 that Jesus and I played football together on the New York Jets. Jesus was a backup tight end, and we got along fabulously. I was a backup wide receiver which meant that Jesus and I got to hang out a lot because we were both on offense and weren't starters. We were each in possession of a specific deficiency and lucky enough to hang onto the second unit.

I was playing behind Don Maynard and George Sauer and Bake Turner, who were all-stars at one time or another, which basically meant I didn't get much playing time. I didn't get to return kicks either, which I wanted to do but couldn't because I had average speed at best. I had what they called "good hands," which just meant that I could run routes and catch well but wasn't fast or quick or strong or particularly athletic.

Joe Namath was our quarterback. He was a graceful statue of a quarterback—thick and flowing. Catching a pass from him was like holding a warm newborn baby in your arms. It was as if he would just reach out and softly hand you that warm, sleeping ball.

The team was coached by Weeb Ewbank, a fireplug of a crew cut of a lump, and I'll tell you, it was really cool playing for an old guy named Weeb. He looked and talked the way a football coach should—a lumpy fire hydrant with horned rimmed glasses, gravel voice, dark plaid dad hat, his fly always down, never moving, yet somehow always splitting the rear of his baggy, unfashionable pants.

Even though I didn't play much, I still didn't mind suiting up for them. We were winning some big games back then as you may've heard and that made things better. But I felt out of place the entire time I was there. New York was just too big for me to get a grip on, and Houston had taken a chance by signing me out of a small school, and then traded me after two years. I was a throw-in in a deal involving better known players. To this day I feel a debt to Houston for taking a chance on me that I never got to pay back. I feel like I never really got to show them what I had. I still think about it quite often.

Nothing in my life meant more to me than pulling on that dreamy crush blue and silver jersey back in all those 1965s that had waited out there for me my entire life. That jersey was holy to me, the most beautiful thing ever—cloudy velvety baby blue sky haze that faded on and on forever. Fade on, fade on. It faded on a dream of blue as if from an eternal sky back home that dissipated into the thin strands of clouds at the sleeves that unfolded back into sky like a road map to heaven, all crisp thin red lines and bright silver.

When I made the team, I balled that sky up in my fists and buried my face into it as if reaching up and pulling it down, wrapping the very sky itself around me. Nothing had ever meant so much to me. I sat there and wept into that sky after everyone had left that first day. I stayed real late, just sitting there on a bench in the locker room in disbelief—afraid to even breathe, not wanting to blow it all away.

When I was a member of the Houston Oilers, I didn't get to play much either, but that was because I was new. George Blanda was our quarterback. He was pretty good, but his passes were stiff and hard. They were more like lobs than actual passes. To catch one of his passes was like catching a heavy melon. You kind of had to run under it like a long fly ball because those cannon-balling pumpkins seldom came right at you, and when they did they sort of wobbled around so you never really knew where they were going to be when you met them, if you could even get to where they ended up.

After I was released by the Jets in '69, I went back to Houston but didn't catch on because they had a rising star at the position in Jerry LeVias. A few years before, when I was with them the first time, they had talked about making me a defensive back. I was worried about my speed and size. I was a little small, but if they didn't put me on the primary receiver, which was always the other team's fastest, I thought it could work out. At least I'd get to play since they always needed help in the secondary. Ultimately, I decided not to switch to defense because my strength was catching the ball, and I thought that's what would keep me in the game. The funny thing about it was that it was a few years later and I was back with the Oilers and they still needed d-backs but by then it was too late to teach me the position. I ended up getting cut at the end of the preseason.

Luckily, an assistant there who really liked me (although I don't know why because I never really talked to him) made a few calls and I ended up in New Orleans that year playing for the Saints behind Danny Abramowicz. We had a decent set of receivers for a really lousy team. We lost big week after week and never got to play on national television, but I did see a bit of action and one game I recovered a fumble from Dave Parks, who was a really good tight end, and another game I caught a tipped pass off the fingers of Al Dodd, another one of our receivers that year.

Our quarterback was Billy Kilmer who was what they called a gritty competitor, which meant he never gave up no matter what. He didn't look like a football player either, not that I did. They said I looked "too smart" to play football. Billy looked like the town drunk, or maybe the guy at the lumber yard, or the shop teacher, or something. Just about anything but a footballer.

For a variety of reasons I didn't do very well with the Saints, mostly because it really wasn't a very good team, and because, like in New York, they had some really stiff competition playing in front of me who had more experience than me. But I had a lot of fun playing and going out at night. It was a good town for that, where New York had just been too big.

I sat out 1971 with a broken ankle. I cracked my ankle in

the last game of 1970 in a blowout loss to the Cardinals. They put me and some others in because why not. Larry Wilson and Jackie Smith dusted me. I had been crushed before, but this one was really bad. I can recall all the times I'd gotten my bell rung, going all the way back to fifth grade—they're the types of things that stay with you forever, as if they're right there in the room with you wherever you go.

We were losing terribly so they put me in on a punt coverage. It was away from the play—Larry hit me high, which wasn't necessarily his favorite place to hit anyone as much as any place was his favorite. He flipped me over and Jackie landed on me, twisting my ankle back. I heard it snap—sounded like a pistol going off in my ear.

I had been hammered before, most notably by Mike Curtis of the Colts—I think I was his favorite target. One time he yanked my face mask around so hard that it twisted my neck and made my legs go numb for a few seconds. I could barely breathe and thought I was going to die. I had never really done anything to him, no eye poke or leg whip. He just did it because I got in his way, although he was inclined to do that sort of thing anyway.

But the Larry-Jackie thing was the only time I was seriously hurt, which is to say it was the only time I couldn't make it back out because I couldn't stand up without a lot of help. My foot just kind of hung there, couldn't hold my weight, so I couldn't stand.

To this day I still believe Larry is proud of that hit. One time he returned an interception while playing with casts on two broken hands. That sort of thing was his job. He was good at it and enjoyed working out there, which was nice, although it didn't do me any good.

I wasn't under contract for the next year, so I was let go. I thought about going up to Canada but my foot wasn't ready. So I ended up back home with my parents where I grew up. I didn't have any place else to go. I ended up sitting in the basement on all those sunny weekends, assembling noble wooden ships on the hassock and sometimes lifting weights with my legs. And although it was 1971, and everyone else seemed to be looking forward to the future, it was still essentially the sixties where everything had been pretty beautiful for me. Except now I was back in the dusty small town that kept me and the faded sun and weeds shrouded in a permanent faded yellow haze that made everything look a lot older than it was. The rich blue-green grass was dry with sad summer songs that whispered to me in the back of my head when I was alone.

I had a lot of time to think, and I started missing my college sweetheart who went up north to grad school when I went south to play ball. She got married a year and a half later, mostly I suspect because she just wanted to be married and was lonely and homesick. Thinking about her now, I realize that I really miss her and wish I wouldn't have let her go. I feel like she has been with me ever since, in all the girls I'd meet and see.

The school she ended up in was a good school—the only one around that had the program she wanted to get into, so there really wasn't much I could do about it. But now I think about it all the time—about what it would be like to be married to her and have a regular life and all.

I wasn't much of a celebrity—nobody could pronounce my name and I wasn't a starter, so every girl who'd heard of me always wanted to hear more about George Sauer or Don Maynard, but rarely me. And since I bounced around, no one really got to remember me—I just sort of faded in and out.

The last I heard of Jesus he was a backup tight end with the Giants—backing up Bob Tucker. Norm Snead was their quarterback until he moved on to San Francisco and Craig Morton was brought over from Dallas. They say after his playing days Jesus is going into social work or religion, which are really smart vocations for a nice guy like that.

The reason I mention all this is because I've been thinking about it a lot lately, especially when it's really late and quiet and I'm alone. I wonder what it would've been like if I hadn't been a decent ballplayer, which is funny because I know a few ex-players like myself. We talk every now and then, but never seem to talk to the guys who still play—some of the older ones still hanging on, but not the younger ones. They don't talk to us much. Maybe they're too busy with it all, I don't know. I guess I recall not talking to the ex-players much when I was coming up. I was too busy with my own stuff, and I guess I figured they had their time and all. I didn't realize until now that maybe they really needed to talk to us some-how—especially the guys who didn't go out on their own terms, like the game still had something of theirs and they figured maybe we knew where it was.

I was thinking now that my career was over. I was wondering if it was all worth it, what it was all for. You're going to think this is really strange and all, but I always figured that if I was really good at something, I don't know, that if I was a good ballplayer or something, that somehow things would work themselves out, that Darla would maybe show up again somewhere. That's pretty weird, I know, but I've been thinking about these guys that come home from the war, or guys who get out of prison after two years and about when they get back home and look around and see that everything's different than what they'd expected, like the whole time, for years, they thought when they got back things would be the same as the day they left. And then they get back and everything is totally different. I want to let you all know, that's exactly how I feel right now.

I always thought how great it would be, but now I realize that I blew it. Now that I've had a lot of time to think, it feels like I had been playing for her for all these years, just trying to hang on for one more season, one more week, one more game—that I'd done my best, and that I'd been a good soldier for her. That's how I feel.

I know you're probably thinking I was out on some macho trip, but that just wasn't me. Everybody was there for the job and because they loved playing ball. It's what we lived for. It was about all I had for her. Hell, it was the only thing I'd ever been any good at—that and fixing cars. I bet you didn't know that you can make as much in *one* training camp as you can in a year as a car jock. It's true.

I ran into her sister in some airport one time. She told me Darla always watched for me on Sundays after church. Those plane rides are long, man. I sat slumped against the window, watching that blue lake of sky, gazing out into that mirror of white strings of fraying clouds, watching for her out there, flying a mile above her city, above her house, above her yard, knowing that we weren't on TV every week, and thinking she had forgotten all about me.

Wasn't I a good soldier for her? Like every catch, every yard was for her—just like a writer with every word or an architect with every line. Walking out onto that field—it's like walking on the moon—not many people can say they did that, you know.

I once caught a pass from Joe Namath.

On and off I played only five years—two each with Houston and New York and that quick year with the Saints. And now I'm just 27. I'd meet people when I was playing, no one would recognize me, but as we got to talking about what each of us did for a living, everyone would always end up telling me how lucky I was. And now I wonder who the lucky one was. I bounced around from airport to airport, hotel to hotel, apartment to apartment—NFL in the fall, winter league, training camps, pulls and strains and deep bruises slowing me down—basically, I was the grunt they sent up the middle on the slant patterns, the guy they'd send to the place where you'd pay for the yard by the bruise—bruise by bruise—and they're relaxing under the shade in the backyard with their wife and kids and dog and grill. They're telling me how great I have it and I'm just thinking—you idiot.

You know how I said that putting on that heavenly Houston Oiler baby blue was the most important thing ever ... well, I've been fixin' to change all that. I was thinking about her—about when I would watch her dress in the morning and undress at night. That was the best. Any fool can put on a uniform. That's what I learned. Cops have cop uniforms, mailmen have mailmen outfits, car jocks have zip-up coveralls, cooks have cook smocks, county linemen have county line-men gear—we all hide in some insipid costume, in our dis-guises. Any fool can put on a tie and any fool can put on a uniform, they don't amount to a hill of beans.

I don't know, maybe I didn't miss much; I do have fond memories of those days—listening to Glen Campbell and Buck Owens and Neil Diamond in the back of my red Corvair convertible on some dirt road that parted a sea of golden wheat and yellow wild flowers, holding some girl in my arms on a blanket under a tree in the country on some late Satur-day afternoon, wearing the breeze as a cool blanket. And play-ing ball on crisp vivid Sundays and having some girl up there watching in the bleachers, playing for her, the field like an ocean when she was a plastic Jesus on the dashboard of my dreams, sitting by the pool in our prolific plaid bermuda shorts and tight fitting striped shirts—miles of stripes and col-ors, flowing on, like dreams.

But now I've been thinking that somehow I should've been with her for all those times. I think about the guy Darla married—I picture him running to the supermarket for milk for her—I picture him being a good soldier for her. I ran pat-terns for her. I ran routes through traffic. I'd beaten Herb Adderly, I'd deaked Willie Brown out of his shorts. That oughta count for something. Shouldn't it? That oughta count for something.

I don't know, maybe I didn't realize then, or maybe I played it too cool somehow, or was too wrapped up in it all—big football star. I was this close though. This close but didn't make it. How am I supposed to feel about that, man? I was this close. Well I tell ya, there isn't even a feeling for that, not anywhere. All I feel is numb—and stupid—and angry at myself because I realize I wasn't there for her. I mean, I ran and ran for her, because she liked that I played football, liked that everyone else liked it. It was about all I had for her, all I could do. I got banged up for her, crunched. I did it because I thought I was supposed to, it was what everyone talked about, what everyone told us how lucky I was to be able to do. And now I have run out of room to run, run out of places to run, nowhere left to run to. And here I sit, still, not even the air moving, the entire world empty of noise. I have run out of places left to hurt.

I'm just thinking about what to do. It's 1971 now and soon it'll be 1972, sooner than I expect, and I don't have one thing to show for it. I have a cool car, and an empty house in a small town. I have the dust blowing through here in waves on the wind. I sent out a bunch of letters, but didn't get invited to any training camps. I even sent up to Canada.

Now I'm just counting the hours, adding them up like receptions, totaling them like yards, each one, one at a time, adding them up to one another—every hour another moment without her; with all those other moments slipping right through my fingers.

There's one more thing that I want you to know now, and that is that I didn't really play professional football with Jesus. I just sort of made that all up so you all would think I was interesting. I did play pro ball for all those teams. I bounced around a lot, even tried the semi-pros and training camps, just about anywhere I could find.

I do want you to know that I didn't make up that one thing about Darla moving away though. I want you to know that I wouldn't joke about something like that, in fact, I don't like talking about it much.

lesser gods

(do you enjoy dressing in women's clothing?)

I was so excited. I hadn't been on a date in what seemed like forever. Then along comes this girl asking about me. And for once some people actually put in a good word for me. I was surprised that they didn't go out of their way to try and mess it all up, spread lies about me and try to convince her not to hang around me. It's an admirable thing to do, to put in a good word for someone. It's the right thing to do. And how many times in life do you get a chance to do the right thing?

When they told her I was single and she should ask me out for a beer or some coffee sometime, she actually said, "Yeah, okay, why not." Can you believe that? And then these people I know actually set it up, arranged the whole thing—for us to meet up later. I was so knocked out by it all, I had to tell someone, but I couldn't tell anyone I knew—I didn't want to jinx it, didn't want to risk the chance that others might try to spoil it.

I was so happy that I skipped the whole way home from work, asking everyone I passed on the sidewalk if I could hug them. "Um, excuse me ma'am, but can I hug you?"

"Hug me?"

"Yes..." I put out my arms, "Hug you. I'm just so happy I have to hug someone right now."

"Get the hell away from me before I call the cops and have your head cracked open." She gave me a suspicious look from the corner of her eye as she quick-stepped away. "Maybe let some of those bees out," she mumbled to herself as she walked off, shaking her head in disbelief, "*Wiiiiide* open."

I got home and wasn't even out of breath from all the skipping. I was so invigorated; it was as if I floated my way home. It had been so long since I'd been out with anyone nice that I wasn't even nervous. I just didn't expect anything of it, maybe a beer and a nice chat, like it was just one more appointment to go to that day, just one more thing to do—cautiously optimistic, but with a sense of adventure.

We met by the fountain in the village square, a very serene setting this time of night. I was tranquil and dapper in my crisp black slacks and dark gray evening jacket. You could've cut bread on my pleats.

The night was a calm velvet blanket that we could lay on and watch the stars sparkle their diamond smiles, as if they were all looking down on us, sparkling their wishes and smiling just for me and her.

She grew out of the evening mist, radiant in her black evening dress. The carriage that was to take us though the park and about the village arrived shortly. It appeared out of the fog like a guardian angel, a glossy bright white and detailed in gold leaf.

As the horse drawn carriage approached, I tried to maneuver myself out of its way, signaling it to stop. But I accidentally lost my footing and slipped on some slush and became entangled in my own feet. I tripped and fell against the horse. This startled the placid beast, and it sort of skipped sideways to try and avoid contact. But as I lunged forward into him, I became tangled in the leather reins and straps. The horse was spooked even further and bolted ahead. By this time I was quite entangled, kicking my leg to try and free myself of the leather web and get myself clear. Unfortunately, my leg became wrapped in the rigging and straps even worse.

The mighty beast kicked and jumped, shaking me around. My arms and legs flailed, slapping the pavement as I lost my footing in the slush again. As I lay on my back in the snow, the horse whipped me back and forth as it tried valiantly to shake me free.

My back and hair became slathered in slush and mud as the mighty horse thrashed me from side to side like a rag doll. I was so embarrassed. It was no big deal, really. I just wanted to meet up with her, that was all. I mean, I didn't even know her, so I didn't know if I even liked her yet. I mean, it was just nice to get out, to not be so cooped up this time of year and staring at the same four walls day after indistinguishable day. I hadn't really thought about it, but I guess I wanted to make the best possible impression I could, and here I was, knotted up under a horse, lying on my back in the mud.

Other people stepped forward to try and calm the horse, but this approach only proved to further worry the beast. Confused, the poor thing skipped ahead, tugging and wrapping me even more.

The driver began unhooking the reins, straps, and apparatus in an effort to untangle us. The driver was a tiny old man who kept telling me not to worry, kept telling me to sit still as he went about unhooking the buckles and straps and reins. Unfortunately, this only freed the horse to go about his business, dragging me by my leg through the puddles of dirt, across the village square. As the people gave chase, the horse bolted, pulling me across the ice and mud and snow and into the wooded park. I screamed uncontrollably "Aaaggghhhhh" as I was rushed along, my back slapping the cold, hard cobblestones, my head slamming, my limbs flailing, the frightened horse increasing his powerful speed, thinking he could outrun me as I flopped, twisted, and bounced—ricocheting off the cold, hard pavement with each bounce, my head pounding the ground again and again and again and again and again and again and again ... bouncing ... scrapping ... slapping ... slamming ... sharing every bounding leap and gallant stride from a truly unique and unexpected perspective. Once in the park, the horse trampled and kicked me as I spun in the muck underneath, kicking up mud and moist gunk.

They finally found me half conscious, lying face down in a ditch on the other side of the park. I had rolled into a stagnant cesspool of festering human waste. They found me covered in every manner of filth—dung, feces, urine, not to mention the rats, mice, and bugs. My clothes became saturated with this mixture of filth. I reeked to high hell.

I came to as some members of a youth club pulled me from the foul, stenchy soup. The comments from these onlookers ranged from enthusiastic awe to simple admiration:

"Cool stunt, stench master."

"Rock on, stench dude ... and then some!"

"Rock on tenaciously! And then when you're done with that, rock on again some more ... later on, at your own convenience."

"That was quite a tumble, stinky."

"Righteous stunt, Stink Man."

"We bow to your grace and courage."

Fortunately the villagers arrived just as the teenagers in ripped denim jackets and black t-shirts were removing my watch and going through my pockets. I remained groggy until I was fed coffee and soup at a restaurant near the village square.

I bent down to warm myself by the great stone fireplace. My clothes were soaked through with a fetid mixture of ripening filth, thus it was difficult to pick out or discern any one specific odor. But it was a powerful odor indeed that I gave off. Apparently, there must have been some gasoline in the ditch that soaked into my clothing because as I leaned in closer to the fire, I went up like an oily rag. Ffffoooooommm! My entire suit caught fire, glowing a brilliant orange as I ran about the restaurant, igniting rugs and tablecloths and screaming uncontrollably "Aaaauuuugggggghhhhh" as I spun and stumbled about.

I peeled off my jacket and flung it away from me. It spun like a ball of fire into a corner and lit up two curtains, then fell to ignite a tablecloth and rug. I pulled at my burning shirt, trying to claw it off my body. I screamed, knocking over tables and chairs as I dashed out the door and into the dark and somber village square. "Aaaaggghhhhhh!!!" I waved my arms and cried in uncontrollable horror as I spun outside. I knew this was terrible behavior, and no way to make a good first impression on someone who actually wanted to meet me, but I had never been on fire before, so having never been so, my behavior was an extension of this new experience, and one I did not handle as well or as gracefully as I would have wanted.

I tripped on the curb and slammed down into the street. I rolled in the gutter, into the filth, mud, muck, and slush, trying to subdue the fire in swimming and crawling gestures. The fire merely hopped from one arm to another—from my back to my stomach—from my sides to my legs and then back to my arms again.

A patron from the restaurant ran out with a tablecloth, another with a rug, trying to wrap me in them to smother the fire. I jumped about going "Ooooo... Ooooo... Aahhh... Aahhh... Oooo... Oooo... Hot stuff... I—Yi—Yi... Oh me... Oh my... Hot stuff." I hopped in circles, frantically patting my legs, my arms, my chest, but the flames were stubborn. Finally I took off, dashing through the quiet village square and diving into the stone fountain. I tore and ripped my elegant evening wear from my body as I flopped and rolled in the freezing water of the fountain.

As I stood, the water began tightening to freeze around me in the cold evening air. The frozen rags dug into my skin. The teenagers who pulled me from the drainage ditch sulked on by, offering their observations:

"Bitchin' sprint, flame man!"

"Nice bolt, Captain Stench! Five bucks ta see ya do it again."

"Flame on and then some, dude." (this one gave me the thumbs up as he bobbed on by)

"Bitchin' stunt... Bitchin'... No way you can top that one... No way."

"Way ta dart, stink man."

"Nice duds, El Stencho."

I wrapped a rug and several tablecloths around my half naked body and crouched by the fire back at the restaurant. The fire glowed on her bright face, lighting her auburn hair to a copper halo as she knelt beside me.

She smiled at my courageous bravery as an attendant swabbed my burned, scabby face. I couldn't believe we were finally alone together.

"So, you're single, huh?" she finally spoke, as if rechecking, in nothing more than a hush.

"Yeah ... I mean, I've met some nice girls before ... but events tend to conspire against a guy."

She smiled and nodded her head.

"You're ... you're so beautiful," I whispered. "What are you thinking about?"

"Oh, me ... I don't know," she whispered back as she watched the fire before us. "I guess I was just thinking about work, you know, just regular day to day stuff."

"What do you do? I mean, what do you like to do?"

"Oh me," she exhaled shyly. 'I'm just a photographer, that's all," she shrugged and looked away, trying to bury her head on her shoulder.

"Wow, an artist. What subjects are you interested in?"

"Aw, you don't want to hear about me," she smiled and shook her head and closed her eyes and shyly looked away again.

"Yeah I do, come on."

"Naw, you wouldn't be interested," she looked down at her feet and shook her head. Her ice blue eyes glowed by the golden fire.

"Sure I am, I bet you're really good. I bet it's some really interesting stuff."

"Well, mostly I enjoy documenting the human condition ... through midget pornography. Hard core dwarf porn. Emmm, bestiality. Well, some midget bestiality," she shrugged. "Lots of fetish stuff—school girls in Catholic school outfits stomping on cockroaches, nude bowling, nude gardening—you know, that sort of thing," she nodded.

"Aahhhh, yeah, sure. That human condition stuff."

"Yeah... I think I'm an okay artist... I'm just as good as the next guy, I mean, maybe someday anyway," she shrugged. "There's some decent money in that stuff. I mean, I can't shoplift and start fires my entire life you know," she sipped her hot chocolate, rolling the mug back and forth in her palms, warming her slender hands. "Now I've got a few questions for you buddy-boy," she reached into the pocket of her little black evening coat and pulled out some folded pieces of notebook paper and began to unwrap them. "Okay, here we are..." she patted them flat on her leg. "Ah, let's see here... Do you enjoy dressing in women's clothing?"

"Pardon me?"

"Do you like to dress up as a chick?"

"Aahhh, not that I'm aware of," I shook my head and squinted.

"How 'bout gladiator movies? Do you enjoy taking in a glad-flick every now and then? When you're just laying about wasting time with your lazy buddies maybe?" Her head was down, reading from the list. She looked over to me, her head still bowed. "Ya like ta take in a glad flick every now an' then, don't cha? Yeah ya do. Come on, you can tell me. You an' yer hairy buddies. Sittin' 'round with yer shirts off. Maybe stappin' on the leather."

"Aahhh, nope," I shook my head again.

"Bladder infections?" She raised her head.

I just calmly nodded no and shrugged.

"Simple chronic halitosis? ... Gastro-intestinal disorders? ... Fish smell syndrome? ... A vestigial tail? ... Anything there?"

"Eemmmm, no. Not that I'm aware of." I shook my head.

She set down the cocoa and pulled another folded note from her jacket. "I write things down," she looked at me, shrugged, then rubbed under her nose. "For instance, here are five reasons why I didn't want to go out with you," she cleared her throat and looked down. "Reason number one: You're probably a loser. Reason number two: You wouldn't impress my friends. Number three: You're not cool enough or good looking enough. Four: You can't read my mind. Five: Since you agreed to go out on a blind date, that must mean that you're a totally desperate loser, tired of internet porn, who can't get anyone, ANYONE, else to go out with you and will settle for *absolutely* anything. Six: You're probably afflicted with some condition, an unnatural immaturity, chronic flatulence, bad taste, bad breath, poor or grossly underdeveloped social skills, public nose picking, etc. to such a degree that no one, NO ONE, else will go *near* you, Seven: Since you obviously can't get a date on your own, you're probably not very bright. Eight: You're probably lonely, desperate, and/or clingy and needy. Nine: I could probably boss you around and you wouldn't mind or notice. Ten: You're probab..."

"I thought you said it was only five. Five reasons."

She glared at me. "Yeah, that's real mature, cut me off. Just cut me off. Interrupt me," she shook her head and looked away. "Already you're not even listening to me," she said to herself under her breath as she stared at a wall in the distance and shook her head.

"Oh, no. No. Please. I apologize. Please. Continue," I gestured a polite, wave. "I ... I was listening."

She cleared her throat. "Reason number ten!" she announced enthusiastically. "You're probably useless. Useless in the kitchen. Useless around the house. Useless in the sack. Can't get the job done..."

"You know, it may not be in your best interest to go around assuming things about people you don't even know, being so critical. I mean, some person may turn out to be ..."

"Number eleven!" she enunciated heartily. "At this point you'd probably settle for anyone. You aren't picky. You don't have standards, which then permeates into the rest of your puny little life... Oh, say," she flipped her folded piece of notebook paper over. "I thought later on we could take this Cosmo Quiz: 'What kind of loser is your man'." She looked over to me, looking me over. "My guess is you're a 'Worthless Loser'... "Eemmm, maybe a 'Pathetic Loser'."

I started getting the sense that she wasn't out on a date to meet *me*, to be out with *me* specifically, but that she was just on a date to impress her friends—to have something to talk about, to brag about, to complain about.

"I'm also writing a good-bye letter to my co-workers. I used to work for a couple of guys, but now I'm going off on my own." She unfolded another note and began reading, "And you, the one I call 'The Grinner,' why don't you brush your teeth once in a while, huh? ..." She looked up to me. "He's the one who has a big crush on me. He never talks to me or anything, but I can tell." She closed her eyes, nodded and smiled to herself. "He's the one whose lunch I always throw away... He brings in a bag and leaves it in the fridge."

"Why... Why would you do something like that?"

"Because he's skeevie, and I don't like him. Duh," she rolled her eyes at me. "He bugs me, drives me crazy... Yeah, he's got it bad for me. I can tell."

"Gosh, do you think those are nice things to say? I mean you might run into these people again someday. They might end up working at a place you want to apply to or something. You really should try to leave on a positive..."

"...And you, the one I call 'Mr. Peepers,' could your glasses get any thicker? I mean, why don't you try some contacts, so your big, sloppy, googley eyes aren't freaking everybody out all the time. And you, the one I call 'racist.' Now I don't know if you are a racist or not, but you sure look like one to me..."

"Um, gosh, it's getting on and all, I really think I should be on my way home. It's been quite a full and eventful evening."

"But I haven't even gotten to the 'Bird Lady' yet. I mean, could she at least nibble on a cracker from time to time or something? Or what about 'Man Breasts?' Could he hit the Stairmaster once in a while? I mean, he must be stealing Bird Lady's lunches or something."

"Ah, maybe some other time..." I stood. "I gotta get going. I gotta get up early and everything tomorrow."

"Oh... Are you sure?"

I drew in a deep breath and looked around. "Yeah I really

should be moseying along. I think I've done enough in here tonight." The place had pretty much cleared out, mostly due to my running around on fire, screaming in panicked terror, flailing my arms and that whole production. The wait staff was mopping the spilled food, folding the burnt tablecloths, rolling up the charred curtains, and dragging the scorched rugs out to the dumpster in the back alley. From time to time they would look over at me and shake their heads and roll their eyes in snobby disgust.

"I think it'd be a good idea to call it a night about now," I looked around. "It doesn't feel like they want us around."

She looked over her shoulder and surveyed the cleanup crew. It was quite a sight. "You must get that a lot, so I assume you're used to that feeling, huh?" she handed me another tablecloth to put around myself.

"Oh... thanks... Monkey Butt."

"Dooooonnn'ttt caaaaalllllll meeeeeee Monkey Butt!!!!" she screamed and waved her arms as an old couple shuffled behind us. They looked over at us and picked up their pace.

"Come on," I nodded to the door and took a step toward the foyer.

"Don't boss me," she stood and brushed herself off.

"Ah, yeah," I stepped to the door.

"Could you, like, stutter any more?"

I stood on the sidewalk outside, hitching up the rug and bundle of tablecloths that now comprised my outfit. After a moment she stepped out to join me. "...and a lousy place to eat too!" she was yelling back at the people inside. She turned to me as she slammed the door behind herself. "You still here?" she snapped with a crinkled nose.

"Yeah, I thought I'd see you home." I waved across the village square to the little man on the horse drawn carriage, the same one who was supposed to show us about. He nodded back and turned to start forward to us. "Here comes the carriage," I pointed.

"Yeah," she snorted, "In your dreams, toga boy," she hissed

and stomped away. "Bag thaaaat."

"Good old Monkey Butt." I sang to myself as she clomped down the walk. "It must be tough being right all the time... What a burden." A few seconds later a snowball cracked me in the back of the neck. The cold snow dripped down my neck and back and made me shiver as it trickled under the table-cloths I was wrapped in.

As I patted the back of my neck to dry the water, I noticed I was standing in front of a barber shop. I slowly turned and noticed my reflection in the window. I stood and looked at myself, waiting for the carriage to make its way over. I looked inside. What a great place—all lit up, all bright and clean, all the shelves lined up, crisp white towels, chrome and shiny mirrors glowing, tile floor, row of waiting chairs, ceiling fans slowly turning. Everything shining all white and silver, like gazing at the inside of a cloud. And everything lined up and in order. Although it really wasn't all that late, I couldn't believe it was still open this time of night... And then I noticed a little blond kid sitting up straight and tall, getting his hair cut. His family was all around him and taking photos, as if this were his very first hair cut and they were making a big deal out of it all. I just stood there and watched. It made me feel warm inside. It made me feel whole and complete all of a sudden. And then, as I heard the horse clomping up, its clomps shooting off the brick of the square, I started feeling a strange little ache of sadness inside, like the ache was mis-placed somehow, like it didn't belong there. I don't know why that perfect little scene should make me feel this way—uncertain, and lost. Maybe I was sad that the kid would have to grow up, that his first hair cut wouldn't last... But then I think of all the great things he'll do—play football with his friends, kiss a girl, build a cool fort—and I felt a little bet-ter... Maybe it was because I couldn't stand there and watch for long, that things didn't seem to last, moments flashing out before our eyes... Maybe it was that I didn't have a kid of my own to take to his first hair cut, and that I was missing out on all those warm things... I don't know why, but watching that little blond freckled kid sitting straight and proud and tall getting his first hair cut made me feel a little sad for a quiet moment.

"Where's that lovely lady you were with?" the little man asked as the carriage pulled up. I had seen him around for years. Rumor had it he was a retired jockey, disgraced in a horse doping scandal.

"Probably out selling angel dust to some junior high kids." I climbed aboard. "Or swindling the elderly," I groaned as I climbed into the back, "I need a ride home."

"Oh, so it didn't work out huh? That's a shame, a real shame," he gave the reins a good tug and the horse jerked us ahead.

"Nothing ventured, nothing gained," I shrugged as I settled into the back seat.

"Boy, that was some night. Some night indeed... I swear, I've never seen a man on fire run like that. I bet those flames were shootin' five, six feet off yer back..."

"Well, I try to stay in shape."

"Take care of your body, and your mind will follow... And those clothes, those were some sure fine duds you were sportin'. Them's gonna cost ya a pretty penny, huh?"

"Yeah, my best evening wear."

"Say, you seem like you're in pretty good shape. I know a sure fire way ta score some quick cashola."

"Well, I'm not sure I need to..."

"Do you like animals?"

"I like animal *crackers*."

"Do you like movies? ... 'Cause I know these people who make cheap films ... and I could sure use a fistful myself this time a year."

"That girl I was with makes movies. Well, movies *and* she starts fires," I watched the trees pass overhead—so slowly, so peacefully, so calm, so at ease with themselves—one by one as we moved into the large city park. The winter trees, each one so stark and simple, twisting gray wires criss-crossing into the deep, dark sky, each so good at being a tree. They were stripped bare of all they were. Exposed. Naked. Alone. They were distilled to their essence, stripped of all their pretense, of all their nonsense, like I wished I could be. And the thin, narrow clouds above glowing a dim silver.

At least you could trust the winter trees. You could always count on them. They were just trees after all. They were all that they could be. They couldn't fool you. They couldn't hide. They couldn't be anything else.

"Hhhmmmm ... fires huh?" he stopped the carriage at the side of the road. "Help me out a minute," he slid off his perch and landed in the grass.

By the time I dismounted, he had already unhitched the horse.

"Help me with this," he was pushing against the carriage as the horse grazed in the grass and snow at the side of the road. We stood under a soft tunnel of frizzy trees in the dark night. The feathery winter breeze felt like a cool stream that ran right though us as we pushed his carriage over. He took out a silver metal flask and sprinkled whatever was in it onto the carriage. "We can say those teenagers did it," he said as he took out his lighter.

The carriage became entangled in a blanket of orange heat. We began warming ourselves by the friendly glow, beneath the calm, dark blue sky. The light blue snow glistened as it reflected the clouds and moon. He took a deep swig from the flask and handed it over to me. "What a night," he grinned as he wiped his mouth with the back of his sleeve.

I stood there wrapped in the gleaming white tablecloths, under that wiry tunnel of trees, in that dark orchid of night, and I thought of how sad it was that in all of this, in the simple, stark landscape, in this simple little world, that all anybody seemed to ever want—all the moping teenagers in black t-shirts, all the conceited waiters, all the bitchy little girls, all the little old carriage drivers shadowed forever by doping scandals, all the cops about to split somebody's head open, all the proud little boys getting their first hair cuts, all of us connected, entangled even, in this strange time that never ends, all the complicated, exhausting goo we go through, all the fragile connections, all the frayed ends, all the tatters and tangles we have to mend, and even in all of that, that it's still so tragically simple that all we ever seem to want is someone to tell us that we're not alone, that we're okay, that we matter, that we're important, that we're not an ugly mutt-puddle alone in a forgotten corner, that everything's going to be all right.

"Sure is," I nodded with a smile, soaked in the fluttering orange glow, as I took the flask. "Sure is a great life," ...I reached down and patted the little jockey's back. "...And everything's going to be all right."

I used to know her

It's Debra now, of course. I should've seen it coming, I suppose. I used to know her when she was just Debby. I knew her when she had all those great freckles—freckles like a field of dandelions blooming across her face. I knew her when she had that complicated smile, a complicated smile like a secret summer morning unfolding with me in the back of the bus. We used to share those mornings, the bus swaying us from side to side. And for a while in those mornings, I had her all to myself—

"I'm probably talking about this way too much, but it's been on my mind..." she always starts sentences that way. I think it's her politeness shining through. It's too bad people around here never see things that way. They say she's pretentious, wordy, that she's showing off. But none of them ever tries to get to know her. You can pretty much count on people around here taking things the wrong way, they just go around assuming things, as if they're smarter than anyone else. It's a lazy way of thinking—making things up, pretending you know things.

"You're thinking about getting out of here again," I sigh, "...off to college. Somewhere in Montana." I finish her thought as the sun brightens her face and the bus jiggles us in the wind, and suddenly she becomes lost in that morning sun, the breeze swirling around us from the windows.

"I just want to be out there. And out of here," she says under her breath, blinking in the golden haze, as if no place is big enough for her. "Majestic, galactic topography, not all flat and nothing, like out here," she extends her arm out the window and catches the morning's cool breath. "I should be out there," she says, reaching far off as several of her shadows appear as fuzzy ghosts behind her.

We sit in the back, the bus bouncing us like an explorer's ship through the dusty hot sun, through waves of green and yellow fields, through waves of empty ground, so many things passing by—stalks of corn, fence posts, telephone poles, old tilting gray sheds, tombstones, leaning empty trees, empty fields, broken trees, hurt trees. No one else wants to sit back here, and they don't want us up front with them, so the back is all ours, our own little sailing ship lost in a wilderness of shadows and blinding sun.

Our stops are at the end of the line, and she gets off before me, so all I knew of her for several weeks was the back of her head and that silver mailbox guarding her long drive-way, waiting for her all day long.

There's nothing out past the last couple of stops—just a lot of flat, empty fields and tilting, gray fence posts. And there's me and her in the empty bus, rattling us through change after change. Over the weeks that bus has become a part of us, and we have become a part of it.

Sitting in the sun of bus, I could feel her in the morning wind. And gradually I could feel my future rushing in that wind. More and more I feel it rushing to me, rushing right past me in a blur. Sometimes I can feel it burning so fast I can't think. Sometimes it feels like it's rushing right through me, like I'm turning into a ghost. I feel the next month in that wind. And I feel the month after that, and the month after that one too, all rushing by so fast.

The end of the school year has me thinking of all of this—of the past and of the future. The March wind blows cold out here. There's nothing to stop it. And now I'm beginning to feel the warm, empty summer in that wind. It's getting so I can sense May 24th and June 6th. I can feel June 19th and July 16th and July 27th. And I can picture August 8th—a cruel, empty August 8th where I'll be sitting on an old peach crate out at work. I'll be sitting all alone watching all the cars and all their lives zipping by in ghosts of blurs. And she just sits there in the sun across the aisle, her eyes closed, the wind blowing her short, sandy hair away from her as she whispers that song, "*Delta Dawn, what's that flower you have on? Could it be a faded rose from days gone by? And did I hear you say you'd be meetin' me here today...*" I can hear her voice, rushing by in that wind.

I first saw her in a bowling alley in town a few years ago. I was with a church youth group. She was with some other church thing a few lanes over. I was standing off to the side in a blue suit that was way too small for me, a ridiculous costume for my age. She was sitting a few seats over. I couldn't take my eyes off her. I watched her, but I couldn't make out what she was saying. Every once in a while I'd catch a little of what she said, but mostly I'd see her in the corner of my eye, laughing so hard she'd be bending over. I'd catch her saying stuff like: "Ohhh, my appendix is acting up again," and moan and hold her side after a bummer roll. "I'm so glad I didn't wear underwear today because I always bowl a lot better without them," she'd say after a good roll. Most of the others around her were very serious and you could tell she didn't want to be with them at all, but some of the girls were laughing with her—mostly the ones whose plaid skirts were very old, or wrinkled, or didn't fit just right.

When they were getting ready to leave, she'd say stuff like: "Hey, who's got the keys? Oop, I do. Oh my, lookie, they're down my pants again. I can feel them jiggling around. Listen. Hear that? Ooooo, that feels kinda funny."

Then one day there she was—on the bus with me. She was one of those exotic girls from another school. Every part of her was fresh and new. She stood out as if she were in color, full pulsating color, and everyone else was in black and white and fading.

I watched her for days before I finally got the courage to say anything. I'd sit closer and closer each day, so she'd get used to me, until gradually over the weeks we were finally sitting by one another and talking and she laughed at my stupid observations about all the stenchy things festering on at our schools, about all the temporary things that didn't really matter. And it got to be that when she wasn't there, when she was sick or something, I'd be wondering about her, about where she was and what she was doing.

"Montana's got these incredible snowy mountains and glimmering golden fields and thick green forests and clear streams and starry skies..." She looks out at it all as we bounce past row after row of corn and wheat. "I want to see what it's like out there. But not that poser ski thing."

She makes me feel so light when she talks like that, like we're floating in the mountains of clouds that roll by above, rolling out to discover new places and other worlds, giant mountains of clouds inching along in the flat blue, entire heavy worlds dragging, scraping by like lost kingdoms, lost friends, misplaced events, forgotten places, places we could recapture, places we could share, empty places waiting for us to fill—until my chest gets tight and heavy when that wind starts blowing and she starts in about moving on, like nothing out here can weigh her down, hold her here, like she's slipping away and I can't do anything to keep her here, like nothing out here is good enough for her, like *I'm* not good enough for her.

At night she must dream of sliding away. Those thoughts must carry her off to sleep, out above all the snowy fields, above all the jocks and cheerleaders, above this flat, blank land. And now all I want is for her to stay here with me in the back of the bus, where we can be alone together in the sun and float in our forgotten kingdom of clouds forever.

Days flip past and more and more I'm feeling her slip away. It's getting to the point that this feeling is all I have. Sometimes I can see her flickering right before me, here in the sun and shadows. Sometimes I can peer into every night of the coming days—days crashing out before me, change proliferating upon change—dividing, multiplying, growing—so many that I can't count them all as they flash by like those leaning, gray telephone poles and old fence posts along the sides of our empty kingdom of road.

It's getting to be the end of spring now. The grass is almost fully green and the sky almost empty of wind, spent on days with her. And I know we're almost out of time. I watch her fading in that seat of hers. All her shadows flicker behind her as she melts into the sun. That sinking feeling weighs me down as she floats past me with an expression that says she's just about to let go.

I don't know what to say to her. It seems everything is changing so fast now, and I have no idea what to do, who to be or where to go. I just wish I could hold it all in place for a few more moments. That's all I want. Just a little while longer. Just a few more moments.

They're tearing down another building downtown. At one time it was a movie theater that I used to go to, and then it was something else, and now it is nothing. They're changing the streets around, they're uprooting trees, they're turning the world inside out. And nobody else notices. No one else cares. Most people don't notice me, others ignore me outright. No one listens. And girls don't like me. Girls don't like me.

A club just burned down—a mythical place people used to gather at and meet other people—a place people shared, a place people like me dreamed of going. And now they're bulldozing it over. They're tearing it all down, rearranging everything. Can't they just leave well enough alone?

"I don't want to see it all go... My life is slipping from me... I have no idea what to do... It's like somehow I'm supposed to know these things."

The stars flicker in the dark blue velvety breath of sky, flickering like they're struggling to snap to life.

"It'll be all right," snaps Jack. "Stay the course."

"Who cares," shrugs Taylor.

"Everything'll be fine, have another beer," advises Pammy.

"Hey sympathy junkie, shut the hell up about all that crap," advises Tim.

The sweet cool breeze blows back and forth in the grass and the stars blink in their soft blue tomorrows. And I lie on my back in the ditch, staring up at it all, but it's all so far away. And I wonder, if I left town, moved on to the city or something, followed after her, if all this wouldn't even exist unless I'm out here with it. All respect to you clouds. All respect to you wind. My arms lie at my sides. I grip the soil and dig my fingers into the ground. So I'm lying in a ditch in the middle of the night. On a *school night* no less. And why? Because there's absolutely nothing else. This is it. And that's sad, but the thing of it is, is that in, like, twenty years I'm going to look back on this and think what a great time this was, what a great place to be—the tall grass blowing all around, the calm, shining blue black sky, the gleaming silver stars, the clean wind running through me as if I'm riding on the wind and whooshing around in the night, in the sky. And I'm drunk. And I've got no place to be. Time has no hold on me, as if time can't even find me out here.

I wake up hung-over again. I'm hangin' bad and the long cool bus ride isn't kind to me, swaying and jiggling and rattling. Even our dilapidated sailing ship of bus is pissed at me, shaking and banging and sounding like it's about to fall apart.

Debby just nods: "Out drinkin' again, huh?"

I nod back, my eyes closed so the sun doesn't break into my brain. Even her voice can't sooth the rattle of the bus as she talks about the colleges she's applying to.

Getting reassured and lying in a grassy ditch drinking half the night didn't seem to change anything back to how it should be. I try to shake it off, but that feeling is still lurking out there, luring me for a moment. Distant chances sparkle for just an instant. Everything circles around, looping in overlapping elliptical ovals, holding me in place. The heavy blue night weighs me down and the changes and chances flicker as the huge orange morning sun flashes on and off in the bus, sunspots slowly moving and merging.

The wind blows hard out here at work. It's too cold in the fall, winter, and spring—too hot in the long empty summer. Sometimes it's nice and quiet, like I've got the whole world to myself, like I'm the only one alive, just left here to read some old science fiction paperbacks I get at the Goodwill. Other times it's so terribly cold and lonely, like I'm the only one left on the entire planet—that I was forgotten, left behind somehow.

Sam, the mailman, is the only one I know way out here. I fill his tank every day at noon. He sits and eats the sandwich he wraps in wax paper every night. We sit and eat our lunches on his bumper, in the shade, facing away from the dusty wind. Sometimes it seems like he's the only one who understands. I used to throw tomatoes at his truck from a grassy ditch when I was a kid. But now that I've gotten to know him, I think he's about the greatest guy ever. He sits and listens, doesn't judge me or tell me what to do, doesn't heap a bunch of stupid expectations down on me. I look forward to seeing him every day. Imagine that, my only friend is the mailman. No wonder she'd never go anywhere with me, some friendless loser like me, some nobody.

He'd been in the 'Nam, but doesn't talk about it much. I don't even know how I knew he was over there; it was just one of those things that you knew about someone, just one of those things that was always out there. But you'd never know it by him. I guess that's just for him to think about, to keep safe, or to keep away from others. I guess he just misses his old friends.

I'm curious by nature, so I'll ask him about it every so often, and sometimes, when it's sunny and quiet, he'll let me into that world an inch or two.

"I was more scared of the people in my own platoon," he'd say. "They were only out for themselves... One night the company clerk stabbed and killed a guy over a card game. The clerk was this skinny, gapped tooth redheaded drunk from

Texas named Rusty. Another guy was cleaning his rifle and accidentally shot a guy in the back and killed him... It was like the Old West out there. Another kid got drunk and stabbed another kid he didn't even know... Everyone just wanted to go home."

"Wow."

"That jungle was so dense ... scary black dense. Like being in a tunnel that breathed around you, as if trying to swallow you... I like it out here—the sparse hills, gently rolling grass, austere fields... Plenty of room... You can see everything."

I look out to where he was looking—a single tree on the side of a grassy hill, a tilting barn in a golden field out in the distance, a huge blue forever sky.

"As far as the rest of it—basically it was like this: we'd be out on patrol—I always volunteered for the morning ones—just to get it over with for the day. We got shot at thirty-one days in a row once. We'd be out in the bush and we'd be spaced out pretty good—not too close and not too far. You'd see a guy maybe ten ... twelve ... not even fifteen feet in front of you, then another over to your right side, and another on your left ... and by the time you looked back over to the first guy ... like a second later—he'd be gone. Just vanished. And you'd never see him again. People would just vanish. Just like that. Swallowed up right beside you. That sort of thing happened all the time."

"Oh, man."

"One night we got shelled so bad that of the hundred and fifty in the unit, maybe half were left three hours later. Just like that."

"You knew 'em all?"

"A lot of 'em," he shrugs matter-of-factly, as if stuff like that were routine, like it just happened that morning.

Sometimes I'd notice Sam shake for a moment. He'd just sit there on the bumper, staring down at the ground and shake. I guess he was thinking about his old buddies back there.

"She's got a lot of good ideas." I nod as I explain to him. "And her colors. I love her colors—the clothes she wears, the patterns, the color of her hair... Her colors. She's got this plaid skirt that contains a color which is that exact magical point where green becomes blue and blue flows into green... That's how I see the world—I see colors." I don't know why I keep dwelling on this. It bubbles up and seeps out like maybe he knows something that can be done, like maybe he can help slow it all down somehow. But all he comes up with is: "Just sit and wait, and one day she'll be right there. Right there in front of you." But I don't believe him.

"There she is," he blurts into the hot air. And suddenly I hear a car pull into the station. I hear the tires crunch under the gravel. A slow purr of engine. A car door close.

I spin off the bumper and lean to look around the side of his mail truck. And sure enough there she is, stepping out of a car, walking to the office as the wind blows in the golden field behind her.

"Flat tire," she shrugs as she spots me walking to her. The wind is loud as it blows her hair around. She waves to her ride and the car slowly pulls away.

"Another?" I shout in the wind.

She shrugs again and I wave her over to the old tow truck.

She reaches out and hands me a crumpled bag from the drive-in down the road. "Toss this for me?"

I take it and flip it into the trash barrel by the pumps as we walk. The grassy fields wave around us. Tan curtains of dust blow by our feet...

"She's got a lot of good ideas. And she's going out to find more..." I gesture, "Ideas ... like nations ... and lives ... crawling right inside of them, going out to explore them, meeting them, working hard, making mistakes, learning, losing, loving, living, not being afraid, getting hurt, taking chances, interviewing Buddha, throwing up on a frat boy, working hard while others sit around resentfully, cautiously clinging to one another, expecting things to just fall from the sky, to just land in their laps, to just be handed right to them..."

"Huh?" Sam the mailman is staring into the distance, into that magical place where the kingdom of infinite sky and empire of fields melt together to become a whole other place no one thought of naming before, a place so beautiful and peaceful and calm that you couldn't name it—a single word wouldn't be able to describe it, wouldn't be able to contain it.

"I was just saying how she wasn't working through anything from her past, or trying to make up for something she feels she's missing, as those others out there would have you think."

"What others? Are we still talking about the game from..."

"Those others ... out there," I point my hand as he lifts his whisky flask. "'Dyke,' they call her, just cause she wants outta here. Who could blame her? She's no snob or bragger ... they make up all kinds of stuff," I shake my head.

"No, no, of course she's not. Not in the least," he wipes his mouth with the back of his sleeve, then wipes his forehead with it.

"Hell, I know her better than that. I rode the bus with her, helped change her flats ... on roads all over these parts. And we'd talk..." he hands me the flask. "...on the bus or in that ol' rig," I gesture the flask to the old orange and white tow truck rusting in the sun and wind. "At least I got to know her before she moves on. Before she leaves and changes ... and changes and changes and changes—overnight ... and every night thereafter—right before my eyes," I look down into my hands, the only things I know for sure, as if even my dirty hands aren't good enough for her. I take a gulp and return the flask to Sam's skinny, shaking hand, "She's always gettin' flats in her mom's station wagon while out watchin' birds and stuff." Sam hands me a sandwich. "People pick on her on the bus because of it—as if they're any better..." A car pulls into the station and honks. I turn my head and yell, "Pump it yerself."

Whoever's in the car shouts back "Aw, come on."

I yell back "Take whatever change off the top of the

pump," without looking over. "Anyway..." I continue, "they mention it at parties, bring it up when she's coming around..."

"Mention what?"

"The flats. They mention the flats all the time, always bugging her about it, rubbing her face in it ... like they're any better."

"Yeah, and if it wasn't that, it'd be something else," Sam shrugs.

"...while I watch her slip further from me... While I'm out off-setting the reducing tee to the flanged wall sleeve... While I'm wasting time reconnecting the filtration return and hyperbolic no-no bar at 30 lbs p.s.i. to the three-way-flange plug valve and after-cooler transducer manifold ... if you know what I mean..." I chew the sandwich and gesture to the huge sprinklers sleeping in the fields like invisible bridges to ancient kingdoms hidden in forests up in the clouds. "It's about my only defense against it."

"Oh sure... Sure it is."

"I'll be stuck taking the flex coupling accelerator off the spool to the uncured core of the jib boom and securing it to the after-cooler at the slide gate while she'll be out losing her virginity to Kikiguard and Hengle during some fantastic ice storm. And I won't be able to stop her. Not with anything. Not with this 22 gauge crescent wrench. Not even with the bigger metric one, the one you have to sign out, the one you have to get permission to use ... the one from that Europe place over there ... the one that'll get you outta just about any jam... And they'll *still* talk about her, as if they figure she's goin' just to piss them stinky townies off, as if to stick it to each and every one of 'em... Who could blame her? Who'd wanna hang out with those bed-wetting, gossipy, do-nothing, crybabies. What've they ever done?"

"Not a damn thing," Sam shakes his head. "They're just jealous that's all. Wastin' time on all the wrong thoughts. Fightin' all the wrong fights."

"I worry 'bout 'er."

"That don't do anyone no good."

"I can't help it. I like 'er. So that's what I do, I worry."

"What's the worst thing?"

"Huh?"

"What's the worst thing you can carry around?"

I shrug. "A death? A loss?"

"There will be plenty of those. Most of those you can't do anything about anyway, even if you think you can."

"What then?"

"Regret... Act now. You're lucky to even get that chance. Maybe you can do something about it. Otherwise what are you left with? You wanna be stuck wasting the days wondering about the things that have no answers? Just left there, stuck, wondering, while life goes on around you? You're just watching the clouds pass, as you say, when maybe you get lucky and can be living in one of them... Every once in a while fate points in someone's direction, some poor bastard gets lucky. It might be you."

I feel the wind running through me. I feel the days ahead. I feel Sam looking down at the sand, sifting through it with his eyes, shaking. I feel her inside of me, warming me, holding me against the wind. And I begin to feel I am the sand, the dust, ready to blow away in the sweeping swirls of wind. It seems the only thing I ever wanted was to be with her. It feels like that's the only feeling I've ever had, the only thing I am any more, the only certainty—dreaming of holding her hand as we kick the leaves in the fall, kissing her and touching her hair and smelling her neck and kissing her soft lips, her warm mouth, rolling around in the tall grass. These thoughts weigh me down, like I'm made of cement, like the sand is finally collecting itself and blowing into me.

The "cool" seniors sign out the conference rooms in the library. They're supposed to be practicing speeches and presentations in there, but really they close the drapes and make-out. And I just shake my head and wonder at how they can do that, how they can swing that, at how they can just make things happen, snap their fingers, things falling into their laps, at how they can make things like that possible, how their dreams can solidify and become physical, become something they can hold.

I dream of holding her in those glowing soft conference rooms, soft curtains and carpet as if in a cloud in the sky, free to float on out of here. But that's me, I guess, always hoping.

I seem to rely on music too much, on the sun, the clouds, the wind. These are just things in the air, just floating, adrift, lost. How can a person stop these things, hold them in place instead of always admiring them from afar? How can I stop her from disappearing? What am I going to do without her inside of me? I feel so empty already—light, like a ghost, like I don't even exist. Until I can't feel anything, only my breath. She's disappearing, escaping from me with my breath, and I feel like I'm evaporating—all the important things that make me a person, that make me *feel* something, are leaving me, leaking into the wind, rolling away with the dust.

Once school is over, I see her only a few more times in the summer. I change a few more flats. She stops in for gas or juice and we talk. I try to call her but she's always out. I try to ask her to do stuff when she stops in... "Say, there's this crappy movie at the drive-in... and I was wondering if you'd like ta head out there sometime?" But I just always end up sitting on the hood of some friend's car drinking out there, staring up at nothing, wishing she was there, as two guys sock away at one another, rolling around in the dirt, drawing a small crowd away from the concession stand.

"Hey, ya hungry? Maybe you'd like ta grab a bite?" But she's always busy. I don't think she catches on, like she thinks I'm just being neighborly. And I just sit out here at work thinking how great the world is, just knowing she's out there, that someone like her is around, as if she were just on the other side of the building.

I feel her in the summer's warm breeze, as if she's thinking of me, looking out there for me. But then it gets so I haven't seen her in a while, and I get to thinking that she's finally gone and how I'll never see her again, how I'll never meet anyone like her, that she's finally slipped away into forever. And in that feeling it seems like my dreams are slipping away too, just flowing right out of me. I can feel my future, everything I could ever think to want or have, fluttering right through me, up from my legs, up into my stomach and chest, tightening, weighing me down, tingling out of my arms and into the wind, twisting off into the clouds, escaping out into the world...

I don't like people telling me what to do, people always assuming they know what's best for me, and yet I need someone to advise me on this girl thing. What can I do here? Isn't there someone I can talk to? A book I can read? A church pamphlet I can consult? Anything to keep my past from peeling from me, keep my present from washing away, sinking into the soil, keep my future out there in front of me where I can find it, keep it all from moving so fast.

I sit out at work, out in the middle of nowhere, on the edge of the world, pieces floating by in the sky, wounds, wishes. I watch the butterflies warming themselves on the backside of the gas station—cocoons and caterpillars growing and changing and living in the wind. And that bright morning sun reminds me of her, a betrayed kingdom we once shared. Before that sun represented potential, the promise of a new day, but now it just rips everything from me. It still feels like I'm being pulled apart. Piece by piece. And there's nothing around to hold it all together. It feels like that giant orange sun of ours is pulling everything away from me.

"She's gone... I know it."

"You're gonna have ta stop doing this to yourself. You're gonna have ta move on."

"I can't help it."

"You'll get over her. You'll meet somebody else. Someone who likes you in that way. You'll see. Besides, I'm kinda glad she's gone for a while. I think it'll be good for ya, give ya a chance to think over other things, maybe give ya somethin' ta work for."

"Tired a seein' a guy suffer in misery and all, huh?"

"Not that, per-say. I was just gettin' tired a sneakin' 'round an' puttin' slow leaking holes in her tires all the time. It took up a lotta my free time."

"You're a mailman—you get full pay for like, five hours of work a day... You did all that fer me?"

"For both a ya... You asked her to do stuff though, right? You held up your end of that deal, right?"

"Yeah, I asked her to do stuff—stuff she liked. I wasn't super obvious about it or anything. I mean, I didn't ask her to 'Blood and Guts II' at the drive-in or anything, but ... well, she always seemed pretty busy, and I figure if she ever ... well."

"You told her how ya felt though?"

"No way. If she wouldn't even go ta lunch with me ... I figured she'd ... An' I didn't want ta make her uncomfortable, ruin the friendship or anything."

"Well zippity frickin' doo-dah, ya little dick throb, ya got nuthin' ta lose then."

"Well that blows!"

"Yeah, well, welcome ta life, pal... Don't get mad at me about it. Do something about it. What else do you see for yourself out there?"

"...I'd like to do a Captain Crunch commercial someday... I think I could be really proud of that... I think that could be a beautiful thing."

"Advertising—there ya go. Ya gotta git yer ass in college, before ya stagnate out here. Before ya rust in place. Like the heeps in the ditch there. Change is good, keeps ya fresh an' on yer toes. No use hangin' 'round here, clingin' to the safety of a past that's already left you behind," Sam scrunches his eyes, his entire body, all dry skin, all elbows and ribs.

"Yeah," I exhale and look down, "Maybe next year... I'm not sure I'm ready just yet." I was glad to hear him pushing me away. I guess maybe I just needed to hear it from someone else.

"You need ta let go. Git into advertisin,' Yer a clever lad. Those guys get *paid* ta smart off. Find your own thing, that's all your own and no one else's."

Then one cold Saturday night in the fall she appears out in the brittle yellow grass at a field party. Suddenly there she is. Glimpses of her jump to me through the crowd, through the beats of music. I watch her as April Wine's *One more time* and *All over town* fade from the open doors of a van parked on the other side of the bonfire. She walks to the fire, orange ripples warming her face, its shadows and light flickering as if ghosts of my past and future fighting one another for space in my heart.

I watch her flashing on and off in the light and dark, appearing and disappearing like a specter. I watch for a moment to make sure it's her, and my heart jumps a few beats, then suddenly stops. I feel numb and everything becomes heavy and it all slows to a stop. The dry, orange leaves freeze in the air. The rippling fire slows, and then, frame-by-frame, heartbeat-by-heartbeat, the flames suddenly stop. The music from the back of Jack's van slows to solid frames, ticking off like flat slabs of heartbeats—boom ... boom ... boom...

"I'm home for the weekend. First time back," she smiles a broad smile to greet me as I step to her. "What'cha up to? Any thrills?" But that was just like her, to say something like that. I thought it was about the nicest thing I'd ever heard, that she'd actually care enough to ask about me. No one else ever bothered to.

"Emm, not much, same ol' shit, I guess," it was so unex-pected, I couldn't think of anything clever to say. And stand-ing there I suddenly felt all warm and solid inside—a sensation I hadn't had in a long time. I couldn't believe she was here.

"Dyke," a girl snaps as she struts by.

"Get a life," I snap as she passes.

"Those narrow minded rednecks have been whispering

amongst themselves, then looking over."

"Nothing better to do with their tiny, pitiful little lives."

Two guys begin swinging away at one another in the distance. They grab each other and roll to the dirt. And I could feel her falling away again, that anything I would say would fail, mere words would be useless, that there wasn't anything I could do, that words had no real purpose, no real value.

"How's school treatin' ya? You diggin' it? What cha' studyin'?"

"It's been great so far," she shrugs. "Big adjustment in lifestyle. It's kind of scary sometimes, everything's so new and different, so much bigger. I must admit sometimes it's nice to have something familiar to hold on to." Then some girl I've never seen before steps up. "Oh, hey, this is my roommate, Karen. We live in the dorm."

"Hi," I shake her hand. "Yeah, that's college for ya, movin' away and all."

"We gotta get goin'," her roommate sweeps her arm across the crisp air.

"Yeah, we're just on our way out, sorry."

"Ah come on, stay awhile. It's early."

"That'd be nice, but she's gotta call home, and we gotta get up early ta get outta here. We didn't even want ta stay this long. We'll talk next time," she waves as she turns away.

"Yeah, I hope so." And just like that she was gone again. I turn to watch as they make their way back through the tall grass, back to their car. And the night becomes darker and colder as I step away from the fire to follow. I could feel her being pushed right past me, pushing fate right up into my face, the town shrinking down around me, the night getting tighter and tighter.

She pulls into the station around ten and I jog out to say hello. Her car pulls up into the gravel, drifts under the metal canopy, the metal cloud. She gets out, her smile a continent of dreams, knowing she'll be away from here soon, knowing all the stuff that's waiting out there for her.

I fill that old tank again.

"We shoulda been on the road an hour ago. We gotta get back. It's a long drive," she sips cranberry juice and leans against the fender's smooth curving shine. Cars zing by in the open plain—one at a time ...... zip ...... zip ...... emmzzip ...... every so often, and someone from one of them yells something as they pass, but it gets lost in the blur.

Unbelievably huge clouds scrape against the horizon, dragging themselves as if they're lost. And I sense them inside of me as I hold the nozzle in the cold morning sun and the fumes cling to me. Her roommate is already fast asleep in the passenger's seat, slumped down, her head leaning against the window, a pillowcase over her face to shield her eyes from the harsh morning light. It is so unbelievably bright this morning that it's like the monstrously huge sun is the only thing out here now, pushing the giant clouds away.

As she's standing there by me, my arms begin to feel heavy and slow, as if someone else is moving them. They feel like a forever kind of heavy. I feel the life in me tingling as it gathers itself to run out through my arms, out into her tank.

"I wish you weren't going. I miss hangin' out with you." I finally say as I return the hose to the pump.

"You always say stuff like that," she smiles and squints in the sun as she hands me a bill. "I like hangin' with you too, but there isn't much else out here for me."

I wave it off casually. "On the house."

"Thanks."

"No worries." I half wave... I could barely lift my arms.

"I'll see ya in a few weeks, we'll talk more then," she smiles back at me as she opens her door.

"For sure."

I lean back against the pump and watch her mom's old brown station wagon pull away. I half dream of her pulling around in front of the station, at first turning in the wrong direction, to head back to town, but then she loops around and back into the station, squealing under the canopy to slow past me, a large sandy dust cloud billowing off with the wind behind her.

"Well maybe you could come up to visit me some week-end?" she slows past me in my mind.

"Yeah. Sure. That'd be great."

"I'll call you," she pulls ahead as she waves out the window.

But I just watch as her car flickers off into the distance, nothing left but glinting silver winks of light, blinking slowly until finally disappearing into the grass and clouds. I am afraid to even move. I don't want her to go. I don't want her to change. It scares me as much as thinking I've outgrown my own possibilities here. And right then I finally realize she isn't coming back. And I feel that change stir inside of me. It peels away from me and grows to form a me that I don't like, a me I don't want. I feel my old life leak out my arms, the old me wiggling into the cold air to follow her, the true me, the best of me, tingling and light, rushing out of my arms into the thin morning sky.

I stand under the rusting metal canopy, the looming metal cloud. I watch the area collapse around her as she shrinks away. I think of how lucky she is, that she thought of something to do, that life gave her that gift, that I was left with nothing, as the sun blinks on and off her car as it shrinks in the distance until it blinks all the way off.

I used to know her. I used to think of her all the time, through the vast dry empty summer days that spread out enormously to forever, carrying her further from my hands, into tremendous solid black nights of gravity, nights of granite that pressed down on you, black nights that you couldn't get a handle on—immense, gigantic nights that probed into you, like a mirror.

how you felt when I disappointed you

I had this friend in high school who kept an old pen up on the top shelf of his locker. We used it to alter our report cards. The school district had budget problems, so all the report cards were printed in a lazy, faded blue which merely required a hazy, fading blue pen to award yourself with the grade you desired. He'd open up the envelope in homeroom and sigh and say, "Yep, looks like it's time to visit the pen."

One day my friend announced he was going out for the football team. He was fast and athletic. We had played basketball together for years. He used to talk like an announcer all the time, but not in a boastful way, more because he'd do these amazing things. He'd even do instant replays every now and then. "Let's see that again," he'd say as if proudly freezing a play in his head forever.

He was damn good; he could be a running back, or anything really. I was kind of jealous, you know, imagining him in that slow motion, scoring touchdowns and hanging out with all the football guys at that pitch dark pizza place after games on Friday nights. He'd have cheerleaders around him and get treated nicely by everyone. His life would be that of a celebrity, mysterious and unpredictable. Could you picture anyone being so lucky in all your life? Could you?

For a few days I was weighed down with those thoughts, my mind wet with photos of him in the newspapers and yearbook, dreaming it was me and not him. I'd bring him along to the pizza place and introduce him to all the cheerleaders, maybe even set him up. But gradually I knew that he would be him, and I would be me, and he would be introducing me to them. I wondered if he'd forget all about me, you know, like a mild cold.

I found out a week later that he couldn't go out for the team. I overheard some guy mentioning it real casually as I was settling down in the cafeteria. He had to work on the farm after school and couldn't get a ride back into town or something.

I sat there in the cafeteria as people came and went, getting up and sitting down with their books and lunch trays and backpacks, coming and going, bitching about some teacher or some girl. I pictured him with those cheerleaders and those touchdowns and those popular people, experiencing those exotic places on Friday nights, being a part of something. He had a herd of friends, all of them pretty and self-assured. I saw him laughing and making out with that Michelle girl, real slowly in the leaves, like golden blankets under a tree in the moonlight, the blankets rolling and twisting and glowing. I felt good for him there, proud as hell, sweating with pride for him, like he belonged there. And I was good there too, cheering for him up in the stands on crisp, dark fall nights. So good that I felt terribly bad inside. A hazy, fading blue sky bad, like I was being crushed, like he had died away years ago and I had just happened to remember him for that moment, that fading moment, picturing him with his touchdowns and with her under that tree at midnight—as if I were reading his mind.

even just for a little while

congratulations

I'm at the bus stop and really hurting. I stretch my back and neck, twisting it all around, trying to work out a tight knot. I've got a really sore neck because I'm breaking in a new set of pillows and thus haven't been sleeping right, my back and sides all stiff now because I laid all night in positions my body isn't used to.

"Oh, congratulations, by the way," a man in an old suit leans to me from down the sidewalk. "I've seen you here before," he nods.

"Congrats on what?" I shrug. I don't recognize the man, thus assume he's got me confused with someone else. Maybe he's just goofing on me because I keep stretching and grooving my back around to try to loosen it up.

"You're expecting," the stranger steps closer to me at the bus stop. He is beaming, "So congratulations!"

"No, I'm not," I shake my head, taken aback, "I'm a guy. I can't get pregnant."

"Oh, you're a guy all right. But you're also pregnant," the stranger smiles without blinking. He's just staring at me—a middle-aged man with a doughy face in an old suit.

"Yeah, right," I look away, turning down the street to see if the bus is coming, "Get away from me, meatball."

"No really. Lots of people are pregnant. Not everyone, of course, but lots of people. Just look around," the stranger looks about.

"Sure. Of course," I nod, unconvinced and now getting a little annoyed.

"Why here. Let me show you," the stranger raises his arm.

"What? What are you doing?" I step back as it looks as though the man is about to touch me.

"It's OK."

"No. I'm fine. Really," I chuckle as I find the situation quite absurd.

"Oh, stop that now," the man steps to me, "No need to be so fussy."

"Why? What're you doing?"

"I'm going to extract your baby," the man shrugs. He looks slightly offended, "Why? What'd you think I was doing?"

"I don't know. Trying to tickle me or something."

"Now why would a person do something like that?"

"I don't know. I don't know you, so how would I know why you'd do anything?"

"Come on now, hold still," he takes a step closer, "This will make you feel better, ease your burden a little."

"What? No. For heaven sakes no. I am not expecting. I'm a guy. I can not have children," I step back, raising my hands to block him.

The doughy looking man lowers his arms. "How can you be so sure?"

"Because. That's just the way it is."

"Why? Who says?" the man raises his arms in the 'what gives' gesture. "Don't you want to see your baby? Hold your baby? Love your baby?" He wraps his arms around himself, closes his eyes, and grins, "You're a lucky man. Lots of people can't even have babies. And here you're all..."

"My baby?"

"Yes. Your baby... Here. Let me show you," he reaches to my chest, "Lift up your shirt. I won't even touch you."

I sigh, look around to see if anyone else notices, but it is still quite early. No one is around. I lift the bottom of my polo shirt, revealing my embarrassingly pallid stomach.

"A little higher," the man leans to me with a serious expression. He crouches to study me. His face grows serious. He kind of does look like a big city doctor from maybe a hundred or a hundred and fifty years ago.

I lift my shirt past my chest.

"Yeah, see. Right there," he smiles and nods in satisfaction.

"What?" I look down.

"There. Right there," he points to my side.

Sure enough there is a little dimple at the side of my chest, about five inches below my underarm. I reach over and feel it. It feels soft and squishy, not at all like a hard lump that it looks to be. It's maybe the size of a pea, like I have a pea under my skin.

"Don't poke it."

"Sorry. Geez, I just didn't know what it was... I was curious."

"I just told you what it is. Want me to pull it out?" his eyes rise to me hopefully.

"Why? What then? Would I owe you money or something?"

"My, you are a suspicious one, aren't you?" the man chuckles. "You'd have a baby. That's what then," he nods seriously, "You want to see your baby, don't you?"

"Ah, yeah. Why not," I shake my head, entirely bored with the conversation now and thinking this will make him go away. I look over my shoulder, wondering when the bus will be here, figuring this is just a gag. Maybe he's a magician and he'll slide a small doll out from his sleeve and try to sell it to me or something. Maybe I'm on one of those hidden camera programs. Maybe he's just bored and trying to make interesting conversation, trying to make something out of an average, nothing weekday morning.

He reaches to my side. I look away, searching for the bus again. I feel a slight tugging at the lump on my side. Then it feels like he's pulling something out. I feel my skin stretch at my side, and definitely something hard stretching and sliding out. I look down and sure enough he's pulling something out of my side—a long, thin something pulled right out of me. I feel a tight tugging, my hands and neck going numb, a popping sound, and then relief.

"There you are," the man beams, cupping his palms together, smiling into his hands, "Oh, look, it's a girl. A wonderful baby girl," he looks up to me, his eyes aglow. "You have a daughter. Congratulations. I'm so happy for you!"

I look down, still holding my shirt up. I do feel lighter now for some reason. I feel different. Better. Relieved. Emptied. My neck and back feel much better, much looser.

He lowers his palms for me to see. Inside his hands is a tiny wiggling baby. I look to my side. There is just a little hole there, just a pinprick, with some pinkness around it, like a bug bite. I look over to the man, then down to his outstretched arms, reaching to offer the baby to me.

"Well here you go now. Take her. She's yours. She's all yours," he giggles in glee.

Stunned and speechless, I lower my shirt, reach down, and slide my cupped hands under the baby.

The man steps back, still crouching slightly, still beaming and now nodding. "Congratulations. Congratulations," he whispers, stepping back.

The baby feels warm. She is naked and squirming around, yawning, with her eyes closed tightly. She is the size of a small mouse, kind of long and lean. I look up at the man. He is nodding and stepping back. A long black limousine pulls to the curb. It is an old car, but well taken care of—shining like a black mirror. A door opens. The man nods and steps back, then turns and walks to the car, climbing into the back seat. The car pulls away and I'm left standing there in the crisp morning air, waiting for the bus, a small, warm, newborn baby squirming in my palms.

my father's secret

At first I just heard the rumors. But I thought that was just people being mean, trying to get under my skin, knock me off balance, take any advantage they could to try and hold me back, bog me down. But then one time at the Piggly Wiggly, I thought I saw a glimpse of him with another family. I couldn't really tell. Then another time me and my friends were riding our bikes on the north side, going to see where some worker got blown up, and I thought I may have caught another glimpse, just a flash as they entered a church. Then riding the bus I thought I saw them in a station wagon. There was a spell of unexpected road work, so the bus had to detour. I saw the station wagon at some obscure gas station I'd never seen before. It was a newer car than we had back at home, and bigger too, but I just caught that frustrating glimpse as it pulled out and turned the other way.

Finally, I biked to that church on the north side, rode all the way up there alone, just to check it out. It took forever to get there. I went at the same time as before when I thought I saw them. I hid up in the balcony, and sure enough I saw my dad with what appeared to be another family, with his other secret family.

During the service I crept around. I was a kid, so who would notice or care. People had their own problems after all, so why would they notice me. I got a good look from several angles. His other kids were younger, so I knew we weren't his secret family, they were. There were three of them, two girls and a boy. They were dressed real nice and were well behaved. That all stung me inside for some reason. But what hurt the most was that he actually looked happy for once ... real happy.

I sat and stewed there for a while. I got mad. Real mad. Madder and madder—at the unfairness of it all, that I didn't get the happy dad, the happy part of him, that I couldn't make him happy. I just figured every dad was like that, but this was proof that it wasn't always like that, that it could be better. And I got mad at that betrayal. I got so mad at him that I crept to the other side, to the pews that were facing where they were looking, on the other side of the altar. I slowly sat up and looked over at them, me just sitting there, taking it all in. Eventually he saw me sitting there. His eyes flashed for a split second, then just looked inward, realizing that I knew. It was glorious.

I just sat there and stared at him, stared at him the whole time. I stared at him good... I stared at him real good.

When it was time to leave, I just left, as if to let him know that it didn't mean nothing. I just got on my bike and booked. I remembered when Alister and Dixie Stubbins' father disappeared, how they heard him sneak out one night, and when a week later he never returned, they burned their family photo albums in the street, that's how upset they were. And that began that rash of small fires—garbage cans, woodpiles, tool sheds—fires that popped up here and there, the same anonymous, squeaky, tear-filled little calls to the fire department each time. In school when we had to draw portraits of our families, they always included a father with no head, or just a wheelbarrow or mailbox stuffed with heads. We all thought they were being too dramatic, but now I sort of know how they felt, as if a strange sickness had randomly leaped from them onto me, drawn by my disbelief, and maybe my insensitivity.

But I didn't want to make any dramatic moves, or take any drastic measures. Not like Stubbins, not like that anyway. I was curious to see how it would all play out, see where it would go. Maybe he was just helping out a friend or something.

It took forever to get back home. For some reason dad was already there, his old car in the drive. I leaned my bike against

the side of the garage and walked in and he's at the table looking over the paper. He looked kind of sick, worn out, and
asked if I wanted to play catch. I didn't know what to say, so I
said sure, and turned back outside. Seems like we hadn't
played catch in a while. Dad hadn't ever been around much. I
went into the garage to get the mitts and ball and there's a
new bike waiting there. I stopped and looked at it awhile. I
reached out to touch it, to make sure it was real. But I didn't
touch it. Not yet anyway. I thought maybe he bought it to
keep me quiet about everything. But then I thought by now
Mom must already know. Adults can sense nonsense. They
can feel it coming on. Anyway, it was their business, their
deal. It was between the adults. What could I do about it anyway, just sulk? What good would that do? Sounded like a
waste of time. I grabbed the mitts and ball and turned for the
back yard. Dad was out there, waiting for me with his back
turned, looking off into the distance. I took a few steps, then
just stood there for a moment in the darkness before the
doorway, slowly realizing that this was the way it was going to
be.

the new neighbors

I've got these new neighbors. They must've just moved in because lately I've been hearing an awful racket—yelling and screaming and things hitting the wall. Sounds like pots and pans. The noises scare me. And the silences after. They make me feel like a little boy. They make me feel very alone for some reason.

These new ones are different than the sounds from whomever was there before. Those old ones were wailing sounds, as if from someone crying out to fate—loud crying and fists pounding the thick old door jambs. And whimpers. Sometimes I'd here a muffled "what have I done?" But the new sounds are mostly things hitting the wall.

I swear one of these days one of them is gonna kill the other. I don't mind the pots and pans; it's the glassware that's the worst. When a glass hits the other side, I wince in a freeze, waiting for that moment, that hanging, empty moment that grabs you before it crashes all over the floor.

I never heard a peep from the last couple who lived there before the "what have I done?" woman. I never even saw them. All I knew about them was their name tag on the mailbox next to mine—it just hung there, curling a sad frown.

I met the new couple down at the mailboxes in the dingy lobby the other day. She didn't say much, just huffed a muffled little "Hi" as he pried open their squeaking little brass mail slot that clung to a single, twisted hinge. He examined the slot for a second, as if searching for the meaning of life in there.

"I hear you're in 2B now, eh?" I followed them upstairs, with the dusty, lazy light dripping down on us from the washed-out golden windows above.

"Yeah," he exhaled as we climbed. She was trailing behind, clutching a grocery bag in a great hug. She was quite pretty in a simple way, with darting gerbil eyes and tar black hair tied back in a short ponytail and a chirpy overbite that sulked under her large, dry lips.

I tried to talk to her, said a quick hello and asked where she was from, where she worked, but she just smiled her tight little smile and shyly shook her head from side to side as we glided down the dirty carpet.

They were musicians—hairy, noble savages, little people with serious pale faces and brittle black hair, and tiny apartment lives of stained linoleum and sick, yellowing wallpaper skin. That was the funny thing about these buildings—they all had the same people, and the same dirty carpets in the halls—carpets you couldn't distinguish any color from—always that blue or green, but you could never tell which because it was always so dark in the halls and the carpets so dirty, and that made everything else seem dark and dirty too, all the light just sucked right into it. Even the air seemed grainy and dirty with its weak light trying so hard. And they all had the same smells—disinfectant smells—terrible, artificial hallway smells that clung to you like a bad day.

I was standing in front of my door the other day, untangling my keys from my jean jacket in the dark hall when a couple of hairy guys with shaggy beards sulked by. They had on fading jeans and ripped jean jackets just like mine. They moved slowly, springing along in a bobbing, skinny slouch as they tried to read the dark room numbers that faded into each door. "This 2B?" One of them squinted.

"Next door," I nodded as they bobbed behind me in the darkness.

"Hey," one of them coughed as I stepped into my door. I stopped and peeked my head out. "Come on over, man," the other one leaned from the doorway and pulled a bottle of wine from an army knapsack. As soon as I saw that I nodded.

There were several people around just like them, quiet and hairy, sitting on painted wood apple crates and an old couch that slumped into the wood floor as if it were stuck in the mud. There were bushy green plants and old floor lamps everywhere and macramé on the walls and a large lacy throw rug in the middle of the room and a skinny blond cat with matted hair slinking around like a long rat. The cat stared at me the entire evening. Everything smelled rich and full, like a perfect barbershop.

All their names sounded very literary and exotic, like a film student's name. But her boyfriend's name didn't sound like anything. It didn't sound literary or musical or artistic. It didn't sound like a fireman or a rodeo guy or a southern base-ball star—it didn't sound like anything.

They all looked artistic, except him. His skin appeared two sizes too tight for his body, stiff and washed out, like he'd gotten it secondhand, or found it in an alley late at night.

I got to talking to this guy who told me about a little trib-utary the city had dammed off not too far from here. He told me about how the fish would get in there and about how they couldn't get back out because of the dam. "Sunnies, crappies, northerns—they were easy catchin'," he wheezed in a dry voice.

Then there was another guy who was telling me about how his neighbor back where he was from accused him of stealing from his garage and about how the sheriff held him until he signed that he did it.

All the while I was watching that girl through the crowd. She flowed so slowly, swaying this way and that, planting her weight on one strong thigh and then shifting over to the other, how she'd look at the floor or off into the distance, fold her arms together and nod while she listened, while she whistled, while she stared down at her small, black shoes. Out of nowhere she wandered around from behind me and sat down on the floor next to this guy.

"Yeah," I exhaled and looked down, "A small town can be a nasty place to grow up. You cross the wrong person and they'll run you outta there with their gossip." I looked around. "A big city, now that's another animal. You can hide in it pretty good, but everyone's just out for themselves here..." I was looking down into my drink. They must have known the rest about being caught in the middle like that because when I looked up they were just looking down into their drinks, too.

"Yeah," one of the hairier ones started in, "Especially if you don't fit in—you're an easy target 'cause you got no click ta insulate ya from alla their monkey-doodle."

"It's nice to be on your own, free and mobile, but there's a disconnected aspect to it, too," someone said.

"Back where I'm from, the insecure rednecks call me a weirdo freak. While around here I'm just a face in the crowd—an average guy. Boring. Bland. Invisible," someone offered from a little circle of people sitting on the floor in the corner next to us.

"Yeah, same here," someone else chimed in.

Then one of them asked about what I did. "I plumb for the school district," I said and they nodded in affirmation as if they'd been under their share of spider-webbed sinks and unplugged countless cloudy toilets themselves. "Pretty much one a yer basic invisible jobs."

Gradually word got around that I was a writer. I was really pleased when they asked about what I wrote. I thought for a moment as I swallowed the raspy wine. "Mostly three page mood pieces, I guess." That seemed to perk them up a little.

"What else?" his quiet, small-eyed girl asked.

"Well," I sighed, "A lot of austere, expressionistic stuff. But none a that self-pitying crap that's so popular," I sipped the wine, "An' none a that smarmy, snarky, oh-so-clever stuff neither. Bad people doing bad things to other bad people... How boring... I don't really consider them stories or anything, they're more like I'm pretending... Pretends... I'm hoping to get them published. Not to impress other pretenders in some stuffy, cold journal where no one would ever see them," I sipped some wine, "I was hoping to keep them together in a book of my own, you know, so people will write good things about me and maybe get a blurb in my paper back home," I shrugged and they nodded silently, as if what I was talking about was flickering somewhere within themselves—crawling through the fog of past reputations and other hand-me-downs.

"Um, what else?" she asked again softly.

I smiled and fumbled for: "Ah, to just be honest, I guess. To report what I see, what I feel." It was the only thing I could think to say. I thought it was sort of—I don't know—uninspired, but she tilted her head and leaned forward just the same. Maybe it was just one of those innocent things you say by accident on average, forgotten Wednesday nights. I don't know, but I was happy she was talking to me. "It's either that or work in the paper mill back home," I shrugged, "kicking out newsprint in huge rolls, like giant toilet paper," I took another swallow of their wine, "I figure if I could get a book together then I could hand it to someone and say, 'Here's what I'm all about, here's what I've seen,' and they'd be able to take it and feel that in their hands."

She nodded with her little gerbil eyes and I passed her the bottle and she held it and seemed to get prettier and prettier with every soft breath.

"It's tough though. Lots of rejection... Sometimes I feel like ... like a clown that's been run over by a milk truck... I try not to let it get me down though. At least I try. That's something, I suppose." I was surprised that they were listening. Their tranquility was comforting. "I want to do something... get out, wake the shadows, wake the echoes, tame that tide of wind," I sighed, my voice getting smaller, more tired, as if I wasn't sure I'd be able to do that—find the time, or know how to.

He hadn't said a thing all night. He just sat frozen, silently drinking and listening to the jazz that fuzzed from some hidden speakers, some hidden jazz that just appeared in the room. He didn't even talk to her, he just sat there—his serious, hairy face hanging off his bony shoulders like a tombstone.

It was nice to talk to some people. I was happy they took an interest in my writing; it made me feel like a real writer. I didn't get many visitors since I wasn't from around here. Most of the people I knew seemed to move away and come back and move away again like some sad merry-go-round, each one fading a bit with each turn. And since I plumb for the school district, most of the people I talk to in the day are kids, which pretty much puts me in the minor leagues of toilets. I mean you know you're someone when you've got someone screaming and banging their hair brushes on the sink while you're under it with their dirty water anointing you. At least you can bill them, so they know you were there, you know you'll be mentioned at their dinner table later that evening.

I was thinking of all this the next day at work. I just sat there, kneeling forward, staring into my reflection in the toilet. I fluttered so beautifully and strange, thinking of all the things I was missing out there, while people milled about in the background, their reflections rippling outside the cloudy window, their silhouettes trapped in that window as if they were trapped in time, as I rippled in the water below, folding and turning.

I was hoping to run into them again back home. I hadn't realized it, but I was hoping to see her around. I caught them on the sidewalk as they were leaving. They ended up going out of town for the weekend, up to some cabin on a lake up north.

I just sat there in my place. God, I didn't like being alone now. It could be the worst kind of torture—knowing I should be out there doing stuff, meeting people, talking to her, but there was no one around to do anything with, no one around to help me meet anyone. And I was kind of mad at her, or mad at fate, or mad at myself for not being smarter somehow, not being clever enough to say the right thing, as if she represented some magic that I was promised long ago. I just sat there getting more mad, thinking why'd you go and leave me here all alone? I sat in my window sill and watched the sky blush from orange to peach to pink, and all the stuff that passes you by. I watched the day fade into night like a deflating balloon. I used to like being alone, but now, I don't know.

That Monday night they were at it again. I heard them in the hall as I was coming home—*clang ... clang ... clang*. As I was opening my door, I noticed theirs was wide open with a brown grocery bag of garbage spilled in front of it.

I walked over and peered in.

They were at the formica table eating dinner. They each had globs of food dripping from their hair and clothes—mashed potatoes and corn. He was staring out the window and she was just sitting still, shrinking in her chair, looking down and sobbing silently with her shoulders curled around herself. There were slight splashes and dots of food on the walls.

I wanted to do something, kneel down and comfort her, but all I could think to say was what was in my hand. I pulled the papers from the folders in my fist and began reading. She was already looking up at me, trying to stop crying. There was an old transparent American flag decal on the window between them, with a plant hanging above it that caught my eye. The reason it did was because there was one just like it—right there between the formica table and the hanging plant—at my grandmother's house in the country when I'd visit in the summer every year when I was a kid. But they never fought, not ever, not even when the bank took their place and they had to move to the city. They never fought once, in fact, they never talked much after that.

My grandmother lived in a little two-story next to some trees out in a field of tall grass. Her place felt like an island in an ocean of golden waves blowing and flowing in the wind. That flag decal reminded me of how my cousins would always drive out there, how they'd always bring their girlfriends to show them that golden sea of grass. And just then I thought about how I never had the chance to drive any girl out into the country on warm summer afternoons.

And now here I was reading to them with blotches of

potatoes dripping from that window and their hands and faces covered with potatoes between that plant and flag decal, as if we were all out in the country, back there on grandma's island somehow.

"I carry these pretends around in a folder," I looked down into the paper in my hands, "So I can look them over and edit them while riding to work and back on a school bus full of squirrelly children," I inhaled deeply and opened my mouth and began reciting:

"He had watched the lovers walk by, hand in hand. He saw them all so clear, as if made of glass. For years he watched from his cage up in the sky as the couples passed on the street below, watching them as if collecting them, a wide assortment assembled by now.

He only had one lamp in the room, an inconveniently short one by his bed that only lit a small corner. Through the window the summer street-light illuminated the ceiling in a golden, murky way—like a soft, distant fire deep under still water. The metal fan on the sill clicked around as the breeze fed it. The floor was cracked and stained, discolored tiles, like an old soup. His black shoes were lined up, floating in that glowing murky soup by his bed. The plastic radio on the dresser waited for the ball game, yet the room still burst somehow with just that bed and dresser fading into the golden walls, and that lamp and radio and fan and mirror on the wall. He had a wooden desk, but gave it to his niece last summer.

He lay passed out with his head on the pillow. One sock was off, revealing his pale white foot, the other sock was crumpled like a Kleenex, several inches from his shoes and an empty bottle on the floor."

Her mouth began to open slowly, like the graceful wings of a small butterfly. I looked at her and smiled and then I turned and walked back to my door.

Later that night I heard her delicate violin moaning tenderly through the veil of wall that separated us. It sounded like breathing. I sat before my old typewriter, my eyes closed as the faint moaning softly rose, whispering like the thin column of turning smoke from my candle. It made me feel empty. It made me feel lonely. I needed to do something, to get out, to go somewhere—like someone was out there looking for me, calling out to me, waiting for me.

I stood and looked across my empty apartment. But I couldn't move. I just stood there feeling embarrassed, ashamed of this place—like any girl would ever be impressed by it. I needed to get out. But I knew nobody was out there. I had already tried and tried. My face began to sting and I realized nobody out there knew I was even in here.

I was looking back on things the other day, bouncing in the bus with all the kids, thinking about the people flying by the windows, some framed in them as we slowed. I was thinking about things—things I had said in the past, things like that. I was thinking about what I had wanted in sixth grade, wondering if I had achieved such dreams, such simple, sunny, back-of-the-bus sixth grade hopes. And I think back and say, yeah, I guess I have—driver's license, place of my own, got out of that small town, moved to the big city, where all the action is, you know, the sort of stuff you dream about on the bus when you're a kid passing fence post after fence post, telephone pole after telephone pole, wondering what you're missing out on.

I sat in my window and read as the sun sank into its sleep. I heard a couple walk by in the alley below. I couldn't see them in the darkness, but I heard them laughing, their tender voices echoed up to me from the alley. I saw another couple touch in the darkness in a window across the alley, their silhouettes becoming one. And now I find myself thinking about that stuff again, just sitting in my window sill wondering why life had a way of making you feel ashamed of yourself.

Finally, I walked over to the kitchen and picked up a bag of garbage. I usually had several scattered about, filled with pizza boxes and empty soup cans. Usually I just toss them out the window and they float down and find their way into the dumpsters in the back alley. Just about everything I have I've found down there—my couch, dresser, end table, book shelf, lamps—all born out of these people, emerging from their arms and legs and guts—as they shed them like fading sins so they could grow into fresh lives.

Sometimes I sit on the sill at night and drop things down one by one—cans and boxes—and watch the TVs flicker in the windows of the buildings next door, glowing on the ceilings and walls of those caves like soft fires, with cloudy shadows stretching away from them like quivering, foggy wishes, all those lives glowing like distant little fires.

I snatched the bag up with one fist and marched it out into the hall without closing the door. He was out there pacing and smoking among his own spilled garbage. We both stood there and looked at each other. He shrugged. "Need a place to crash tonight?" I offered.

He looked back over his shoulder to his door, then back down the hall to me and nodded. I swung my arm around and flung my bag over to theirs and waved him down. He shuffled in cautiously, at first just holding himself in the door for a split second and then stepping in as I gestured him over to the couch. It was an impossible couch, limp and stubbornly uncomfortable, collapsed in a permanent sag as if passed out drunk. It had four old bricks for legs and smelled of beer and long nights. He slid into it as if born from such couches. I tossed him an old blanket. "A new place might take your mind off things."

He slumped down and stretched his legs out as he tried to cover himself with the small blanket, and her violin's smoky moaning appeared from the wall as a murky apparition.

The next morning I was standing in the kitchen and looking out to see what it was like out, like I do every day. The sun was bright—harsh and abrasive against the tiny window. So much so that it frightened me. It meant I would have to go out and get in it all again—like all those others out there having a good time, with things to do and people to hang around with, like some wonderful beer commercial. Life. What a mirror. And I didn't want to look. I just stood there, feeling the shame of the wind, with no one here to share it with or lean it on.

At least the sun was up. That was something. At least I

had that. The sky was clear with a weak blue and the birds were chirping. I looked down into the neighbors' backyards across the alley. One of them had this giant patch of yellow flowers spread out against a little leaning garage. The tiny garage looked as if it were still asleep. I looked out on this every day—to check up on this one purple flower growing in that little patch of yellow.

And as I looked down to the tiny back lawns, I saw her standing alone in one. She was wrapped in a thin bathrobe, bent over picking tomatoes from the neighbor's garden. The robe was wrapped around her so tightly that I could see every detail of her curving body, every bone, every muscle, every possibility. She was beautiful in that garden, like she belonged there, as if she had grown out of it.

The garden was hidden from the alley by tall bushes, but from up here you could see into it perfectly. You could see into the backs of those sad little houses. You could see everything.

Suddenly an old lady shot out the back door of the house. The screen door cracked silently against the siding and she began yelling and pointing to the alley. His woman in her flimsy bathrobe straightened up and threw a tomato at the old lady, then turned and jumped through a crack in the bushes. She landed on the wet concrete of the alley and ran to the back door, an armful of vegetables embraced to her chest as she was expelled from the garden.

I turned and looked at him. He was lying on the impossible couch. It sagged under him, uncooperatively forming to his curve. He had his back to me, with the thin blanket just big enough to cover his midsection. He rolled over, and then back again in the forgiving, sympathetic morning light that touched him from the window. I watched him breathing heavily, heaving up and down, and at that moment, glowing in that tired, hazy light, the sun anointing him from above, I regarded him as the luckiest man I had ever set eyes on.

silhouette

(several vignettes with sudden endings)

dry afternoon

She stomped out without a word, down the worn, faded back steps, across the dry, cracked street, and straight into the supermarket. The heat slapped the screen door, stopping the slap dead in the still, shallow air.

She stood stiffly in the cold of the produce section. The produce man in his white apron hosed off the lettuce. The cold licked up her arms. It rubbed under her chin.

A muddy faced kid in dirty clothes stood alone, bawling loudly a few feet away.

She leaned against the side of the cooler, with one arm supporting her in the mist of crisp, moist air. She flipped the pages of a fashion magazine from the magazine rack, trying to forget about him and that baseball game of his up there.

she broke it to me quickly, after she had been out drinking, like I always thought she would

"Okay, okay," was about all I could think to say. I should've been better prepared for this moment. There had been some close calls, but this one took me by surprise. I guess I just wasn't ready for it yet.

She was standing in the doorway. She was swaying, pieces of her body moving without thought. The door was wide open into the dark hall.

I rose from her mattress that lay tilted, spinning in the room with the tattered blankets spilled out all over the floor pushing away scattered clothes and ripped old books. I rose, leaving the book I had almost finished.

The weight of the moment began sinking in, growing on me. My legs weakened and I slowly began sinking to my knees as if I were melting into the floor. My arms tingled, then became numb, like a light going out. My throat evaporated to dry rust. The air stopped stirring. The air became dry and heavy and gritty too. My legs felt all noodley, as if liquefying. The hard wood floor stung my bare knees as my weight pressed down upon them—as all the weight pressed down.

I couldn't breath. I tried to gulp some air, tried to say something, tried to speak, but nothing was there. It was all gone now, my past and future were changing.

She turned her back on me and walked into the bathroom and unclipped her earrings. I turned away from the bathroom door, listening to them clink clink into her ceramic bowl by the sink. I just stood there for a moment listening to the echo ring. Finally, I reached over and pulled my quilt up, the light blue one my grandmother made. I rolled it over and over in my hands—too many times. The quilt was stitched together from pieces of old blankets and old clothing, from old times I remember, and those old places and times spun as I rolled them up in my arms.

I looked over at the mattress on the floor, such a simple thing. My almost finished book was now lost in the tangled rags of blankets.

"Why... Why don't you like me anymore?" my voice cracked. My voice always quivered and cracked at this moment, as if I would have to go through this same thing with everyone I'll ever meet. There was a long silence, but I persisted. "Why?" There were tears in my eyes and my voice creaked more.

"I don't know," she finally sighed, not even looking at me. "I ... I just don't."

I sat there, numb and empty all over. "I guess I can get the rest of my stuff tomorrow," I said, hitching up the blanket under my arm and searching the floor, trying to see more of my things, wishing I had more there in that $285-a-month one room.

"Okay," she said leaning against the bathroom door as I stood and turned to the hallway. The door to the hall was still wide open, but now darker than ever.

I had a bad feeling—that this was how it was going to be... If not for... Well... it was just the way they smelled when they leaned in so close... Everything would be so much easier if they just didn't smell that way...

the bright, early morning of a very long, empty day

I could still smell him in the room, on my body and on my sheets and blankets and pillow. I could feel him here as I climbed out of my pajamas.

That ring we got at the pawn shop was next to me, lying on top of my grandmother's dresser. One of his work shirts hung on a wire hanger in the window, swaying in the morning's breath. It glowed an angelic, luminous white in the warmth of light shining through the veil of trees rubbing against the house.

I wished I could give him everything, I really do, but I can't even find what I want—whatever that could be.

And then I heard him, his tires crunching under the soft gravel.

I could barely see his car pull up. I watched from my window, my head swaying, searching for a better view through the leaves and shade and his shirt. He pulled into the driveway lazily, and his car spit him out and he slipped under the leaves and into the black and white pitter-patter of hot and cold sun and shade. The air filled with circling thoughts, and all the sentences that never get finished.

And at that moment the world stopped with an abrupt

halt, and I felt my life come to a screeching end. And then I felt two things: 1) By the way he quickly, carelessly half-parked, with the front half on the grass and the tail end sticking out into the drive, I could tell this would be the last time he would ever drive out this way. And 2) I knew I never wanted to feel this alone ever again.

I thought inviting her over would be the polite thing to do

Maybe it was better to just say hello, how are you, good luck, good bye, and move on, but she always did like my spaghetti...

"I see you still have that chair," she said smiling in the sun. The window was tall and thin, a small view of the driveway two stories up. The chair sat in front of it with a great view of all the jagged, colorful roofs and treetops that spread out as far as the eye could see. Red and green roofs. Gray and black roofs. A patch quilt of lives out there.

"That's your chair," I pointed while scooping the noodles. I was balancing the plates in my hands, standing across the room, the sun at my feet.

She was looking at the chair, sitting on the floor between me and the chair. Her back was to the door and to me, leaning more toward the chair but still looking back over her shoulder a bit at me.

It was worn and secondhand. She had stitched it up when we first got it. I re-nailed the arms.

"No, it's yours," she said plainly. "You fixed it. You fixed it up."

"You paid for it," I said.

We were eating and watching TV so she didn't say so much after that, I mean she did say she couldn't stay long. After she left, I wiped the dishes and set them back on the shelf, then I walked across the empty room and sat in that chair for a while. I watched the city, the roofs and the breeze blowing patterns in the trees, knowing she was out there somewhere.

lives of shallow murky gold

I got a call from an old friend late last night. I knew him for a while in grade school and then he moved away and I never saw him again. Gosh, I hadn't even thought of him in years. I remember a bunch of us used to play football all the time. We used to go down to the banks of the river and play army. We used to throw acorns at girls. We used to do all manner of kid things, guy things.

It was about 11:30 at night and I was ironing some pants and drinking a Surfers on Acid and listening to some old tapes—the Screaming Blue Messiah's *Clear View* and the Hoodoo Gurus *Death Defying* and The Magnolia's *Walkin' a Circle* and The Replacements' *Left of the Dial*. The cold spring wind blew against the window and the deep blue night churned with purple currents that made it feel like an ocean, and that I was looking down on it from above. And for a long while it felt like I was alone in a vast sailing ship, lost up in that quietly folding sky.

"Hello," I answered. An old western was on the TV, Gunsmoke or Bonanza, one of those shows we used to watch a long time ago when we were kids, a long time ago when we were free, free from lonely thoughts. The color was all soft and washed out and the volume was down. Little Joe, or some such childhood cowboy, was riding off into the long grass on a bright sunny cowboy day.

"Ah, hi. This is Vern Bernbernbernbern, from Campus Lab. Do you remember me?"

"Yeah, ah, hi Vern, I remember. How's it goin'?" I sipped my drink and circled the iron.

"Remember that big pile of tires we used to play on? And making forts in the hay out in the field?"

"Yeah, sure Vern, I remember..." my voice was quiet and

even, trying to calm that wind. "...Out by the granite sheds."

"Yeah, ah, they burned down. The tires did. About six years ago... In the middle of the summer. They burned for a week."

"Ya don't say. Hmm, that's a long time ta burn, Vern." I stopped moving my iron around.

"Anyway, I know it's late... I just thought you should know."

"Oh, gosh, that was nice of you. Was there anything else, Vern?"

"Ah, nothing else... Um, I was just wondering ... I was wondering if you still needed me?"

The cold spring wind scratched against the window. And one of those songs hummed gently in the near distance.

I though for a moment, as the smoky sky stirred, looking down on me with contempt. "Of course I still do, Vern, of course I do."

"Oh, ah good... Well, good night."

"Good night, Vern," and I set the phone down and continued to iron, swirling the iron around with the rolling clouds above and the wind in the grass.

It was late as hell by the time I finished ironing the pants. But I still put on my jacket and walked outside. The cool wind was blowing strong. I stood and looked up at that dark sky, almost challenging it. And as I stood there, I wished I had said more to Vern. I wished I would've said "Of course I still miss you." It's been years, and I miss my friends from long ago more than ever now. I stood there for a while, then I walked out to the tall grass at the edge of the field. I began walking in the field, walking a curving path out into the straw, working it down, starting to carve out a fort as an old record hummed quietly in the house.

you're a rippin' (borderline paint-sniffing) poet, dude

in the morning some children skip by a stuffed yellow duck that is lying in the blue street. the blue tires of cars are flowing around like water to avoid it. the sun is bright and attentive, and somewhere else blue rocks are getting pelted by an old evenrude's propellers operated by an old man in fishing gear in a misty blue morning in a flat mirror of dark blue water.   and a neighborhood girl I like is barely visible. she is walking away. down the street. through a small window.

and in seeing this in the street in the morning, framed in the small window of my basquiat cage, i wished that i was a big big star. so that girls like that and people would like and appreciate me. someday, maybe. i'll show all you dickheads. 8. but i just want to be left alone for now. 4. i pull the covers up, over my head. And I think of how i'm going to get out of here someday. i'm going to work really hard and i'm going to change, God, for once in my life i'm going to change and i'm going to work really hard—really hard. [and i think it's so sad that all of these things are just thoughts, just words.   and small words at that.

remember them.

lovers at the observatory

in the morning some children skip by me. i'm barefoot and shuffling down the street in my torn and dirty pajamas. "be gentlemen, assholes," i mumble as they skip by. they turn and look at me and then run away giggling. i continue shuffling down the walk, under the canopy of bright green leaves.

we used to play wiffle ball in the expansive dirt yard behind st. john cancious church, in the center of the worst part of town. a high chain link fence encircled it like a protective castle. the blue tar streets gleamed like a moat in the endless sun and the world moved around us—all blue sky and green grass. and we'd drink our precious few stolen beers and watch the troubled people escape from the big clean white halfway houses across the street as big clean white clouds forced themselves by, and big clean white attendants chased after.

and we would stop our games and sit in the dirt and grass and sip our beers that unemployed older brothers who hung out at the gas station provided and we would watch the troubled break free, as large clouds forced themselves into our blue and green world.

as i sat in the sand i wondered if years later i would be gazing out one of those windows, through the trees and across the street at the children standing around, sitting on the bench, waiting for their turn.

occasionally we'd hit that cataclysmic home run that would sail over the castle wall and across the moat of street and into the clean crisp green lawns of those big white houses, as if falling through time. but we'd never run after any of those home runs. we'd all stop and look over at them for a moment, as if the entire world had come to a sudden end at that instant. And we'd always just leave them there, as large clouds forced themselves into our world.

silhouette

"Jacky, do you think we'll be friends when we're older?" I said in a whistle, flatly looking past his girl and into his face.

Jack chewed this a moment, rolling it over and over in his plain stare. "Why not," he shrugged.

People were buzzing around the couch with their "Oh hi's" and their "I like those shoes." But I couldn't make any of them out as they were diffused in the dim light that back-lit them from the yard, blotting them like paper dolls into pale, looming, overcast shadows.

I exhaled, "I don't know," and shrugged.

I looked up at everybody. "I just had this feeling, that's all. Just a passing feeling." Everybody looked so strange somehow as they circled in front of the picture window with the light flickering in from the trees—like the fuzzy and buzzing grainy furry of an old filmstrip from third grade—flat with too much fading color, too much forgotten color—too many things forgotten. God, I haven't seen a filmstrip in years.

They sat across from me like tragic ghosts, like fading suggestions of old heroes. They didn't sit all that close, but they were close. She lit up and leaned forward, putting her elbows on her knees, close together, then set her chin into her cupped hands. She blew air out of her mouth and shrugged and her eyes got bigger.

"Well, you've got a lot going on and all..." I explained, still trying to hold onto things somehow "...It's all bound to get in the way some."

They didn't have any response to this, nor should they I guess. They just sat there plain and still, like fraying cardboard with fraying cardboard lives. You take them out of the closet every now and then and somehow they manage to get themselves banged up some. But you don't really notice it all that often, that cardboard getting passed on and on and on.

I sat back, watching the others, their lives like their silhouettes in the window, milling about behind the couch—circling and swirling, clinging to the air like the leaves outside, clinging to the wind—like me.

the knockout

I saw this girl today who I haven't seen since grade school. She was always really smart—math, orchestra, that sort of thing—couldn't catch a baseball to save her life though. She'd always sit alone in the front of the bus. She'd vomit up there every so often, on hot sunny days, probably while I was in back with my friends, dreaming of wading in the deep grass, a baseball frozen a dozen feet before my hands.

I saw her at a lecture at the college today. She's a total knockout now. I still can't believe my eyes. She's full of smarts—full of smart things, smart boys probably hassling her, all the time trying to keep up, everyone trying to get close to her. It looks like the smart thing to do.

Funny thing—I never really got to know her. She was in band, I was in sports, and that's all they had me do. It wasn't that I wasn't exposed to other things, I guess my mind was always just on sports, on what came naturally to me, so that's how I saw things, the only language I could speak. Everything else was just a blur.

Talking to her now, I feel like the biggest loser ever. So I can catch a baseball; it's about all I can do. She stands there talking, leaning, stretching against the railing like a cat, her lovers drifting by like lost ships, forever circling, searching for her bright kingdom.

I'll tell you this has happened lately, whenever I've been talking to some knockout some other guy always happens along and aces me out. Usually he's a test pilot, an astronaut, a war hero, a composer, a 16th century French playwright, someone like that. And all I have is a baseball, frozen in time, just within my reach.

We were chatting and sure as the day, one of those guys

approaches, her friend, one of thousands I suppose.

He is immaculate in appearance, supporting the wisdom of Euclid in his wavy dark hair, the insight of Ibsen in his square jaw, a lifetime of deserts and proud old oaks tucked away in his steely glance, the sensitivity of 500,000 glowing white rabbits in his soft, cloudy gray gaze, and the bravado of a handful of bullfighters and a half dozen mountain streams encased in his gentleman's frame.

She gives this world meaning in truth and beauty. He's probably an architect, a deconstructivist, a dadaist, a mathematician/test pilot, specializing in number theory and higher order thinking, some swashbuckling pirate who has seen everything there is to see, been everywhere twice, maybe a member of some tactical SWAT team on the side—just for something to do.

His suit is mythical—straight, lean, long, pure, giving, musical, thoughtful, caring, dynamic, cosmopolitan, unselfish, strong, industrious, and nostalgic for his mother, her peanut butter cookies, and snowy Christmas mornings. He's probably even got a cool name—like Josh Paskowitz or Pepper or Tino or Vince or Chad or Luke or Doug.

I just stand there in my t-shirt and jeans, shaking my head in disbelief. I don't even know *one* nice girl. I can't even look at him. I want to see his magic suit fuel all the jealous fires of hell. But I know somehow, somehow if he were there, in all the farthest places from her, in all the dark, dank places, he would probably search out and gather up all those lost souls, sheltering them, assembling a beautiful choir out of their restless, ashamed eyes. They'd sing Italian serenades, her favorites, with a tenderness of all the sleeping puppies at the ends of all the lonely girls' beds while they fumble after baseballs and sit alone in the front of the bus, even in their dreams.

He wanders down the steps to find a seat, his forest of a hand running down the river of her arm to catch the sky of her eyes and turns after wading in those deep eyes. She releases him and looks softly back up to me.

I'd like to pay someone to make him look like a wussy. I'd

like to see him knocked out, so he knows how it feels. These thoughts go screaming by, but I can't even catch them. Why can't I ever be like that, God? Why have you only given me that baseball?

Looks like it's up to me, but man, I'm full of that—talking to some knockout and some slicky boy has to come along and spoil a perfect moment I could have stored up and saved for all the times I'm weak and haunted and the days are making fun of me.

I can only dream of such a good thing, of saving up the time I talked to her for that one beautiful moment. Such a majestic thing, as she looks into my eyes and I'm just stuttering, asks how I'm doing and I'm too mesmerized to close my mouth, only to have her look past me to him, glowing of brooding philosophy, slick hair, wine and candles and opera and French dinners. And I want to die. I hate this. I want her. I hate this. She wanders down the stairs, saying her good-bye with a quick wave swimming in her tide, glowing in the last of her sunsets as I fade on, a quarter mile with each slinking step, drifting away, falling from her life.

All I can do is offer some sad, slight smile, and exhale all the hope in me and mouth "Damn." It's that ancient riddle: how do you make an impression on a girl in ten seconds or less? And I'd swear by the hair on my palms that she's the prettiest girl ever.

To try your hardest, that's what you do. You try and try and try. But of all the small victories and of all the small defeats, these are the most beautifully painful.

modern problems (part 364,927)

I surveyed the mess that was my dining room, the mess I had made of my life.

"No one should live like this," a whisper escaped as nothing but a slight wheeze, a resigned sigh. It was cleaning day again, more hours lost to the dusting and vacuuming and dishes, in a further bid to become the most boring person alive.

I didn't even know where to start with all the crap that had piled up. So I turned and walked outside, heading to the library. I strutted down the walk and past my neighbor, Ekborg, who, even as an adult, looked like every kid you ever went to junior high school with. I nodded as I passed and whispered "Hey." But Ekborg only threw me some shade, as always, still steamed that I "only" spent an hour-and-a-half at his barbeque last summer.

I stomped the few blocks to the library.

(thought #83—I thought about shining Ekborg on, being super nice, but then remembered that people around here often wasted their pleasantries on all the wrong people... Plus his apartment felt contrived, like it was all bought from a catalog. There was nothing of Ekborg in there. It looked like a show-room, devoid of humanity. It made me grateful my place looked like the back of an old country gas station)

Up ahead was Emberg. I tried to wave but she passed in front of me onto a side street. Now her place felt like a home. She had a good balance there, and it always smelt like your friend's grandmother's house the day before Thanksgiving.

At the end of the block a bus passed in front of me. I caught a glimpse of my reflection in the windows.

(thought #84—Every now and then I'll catch a glance of

myself, and sometimes I'll look real good—hair in place, clothes that fit, in style, in order, not frayed or faded—but on those rare occasions I'll feel kind of bad because I'll have no place to go, no place to show off to. For example: in this instance I'm going to the library, and no one I know is ever there but those poor lost souls who have nothing better to do, no better place to be. And I am one of them. Seems my whole life I've spent waiting, waiting for someone or some thing to show up, notice me, spirit me away on some adventure. But I'm alone all the time. It never happens. No one ever seemed to notice me)

(hunch #28—I caught a small, faint flash in the corner of the sky, way off in the distance—just a silver glint of a reflection in the pale blue. Probably just a lost jet liner. Or maybe a UFO surveying the area, checking things out, keeping tabs on us. We're probably just an old penal colony of theirs anyway, their equivalent to our Australia. Yeah, they're probably just checking up on us. Man, are they gonna be disappointed with what we've done with the place while they've been away.

I wonder if God would confine his or her infinite imagination, creativity, artistry, and poetry to just one sad little corner of one forgotten solar system, and then call it a day, or if he or she would spread it around some. And if the aliens really did create us, as some experiment, or some hobby to fiddle with, or just some random amusement while they were bored, or riding out a deep bummer or something, then who created the aliens? Who created the creators? Who allowed it all to blossom? Who sent them? And where the heck have they been after they stirred the pot and then just left us here?)

I noticed someone standing in a window of an apartment. It was a lying weasel gazing out at me with a mischievous smirk, chomping at the bit to get out there and lie about me, you, and anyone else.

(suspicion #362—Yeah, there's at least one insecure liar in every crowd, a misery merchant looking to cause problems, then denying it. And when you call them on their lying, all they can do is shrug and blame you for it, saying "Ah, come on,

man. Be cool, man, be cool. I was just joking, just kidding around. What? Don't you have a sense of humor?" as if to blame you for their need to ruin everything. And that's what they want from you—your attention, to draw you away from anything that might advance yourself, to waste your precious little time. The worst thing you can do to them is deny them their perceived and self-appointed authority over you. They try to assign their own values to you. And if you don't fit that template, then they have to label you crazy, lazy, hazy, etc. Too bad that's their only talent—trying to ruin everything. They try to convince everyone that you're a failure. Sometimes their rumors and misery lingers, and the "feel bads" follow you like a fog, lingering to haunt your days as weak puppets echo their lies, spreading the misery, setting up obstacles, hogging resources, elbowing others away from you. They seem to feel this is an accomplishment, that they are actually doing something by getting in the way. They cause problems to feel productive. It's their contribution)

(weird sensation #86—All of a sudden, I thought it was odd that I didn't have a girlfriend. I guess I was too busy trying to get by, make a living, make something of myself, contribute to society, or too busy vacuuming, ironing, running errands. Paradoxically, I cleaned and groomed in order to be presentable in the hopes that maybe I'd attract someone nice (underline the qualifier "nice" a couple billion times), yet I was so busy with work and cleaning that I didn't have time to attract anyone nice, or too focused to notice anyone. I know how sad the situation is, how hard it is to find someone who also desires an uncluttered life, who longs for the idea of space and room—room to breathe, to contemplate, to brood, to create—space for possibilities. Clutter is finite, it blocks your view. Expanse allows space for possibilities, and time to expand. But sometimes that's all I think my existence is about—just cleaning—all I'm good for, all you could ever expect from me)

(recollection # 213—I remember as a kid every once in a while they made us sit around in a circle and they would ask us *what we wanted out of life. The kids would go around in order, one by one: to be a good baseball player, to have a Winnebego Tonka truck, to build a cool fort my brother couldn't find and ruin, to have a magic pony that could fly, to have my parents get back together, to be good at math, to have Geraldine be my girlfriend—and I would always report: to have my head not hurt all the time, to be free of the pain. They would ask about our fathers and the kids would respond: tall, fat, busy, sleepy, hairy. And I would add: unfathomable)*

(weird sensation #87—I had that dream again last night—the unwritten dictates of society prompted me to get my apartment. I moved in and discovered over time a small door inside the cupboard under the sink. I didn't think about the little door much, I guess I just figured it was an access panel to some dumb plumbing pipes and valves. Until one day I felt compelled by some ancient urge to crawl under the sink and open that little door, where I found a small, narrow room, the size of a long closet. I found this situation too curious not to investigate, so I squeezed in through that narrow little doorway, and stood and looked around. I found the smallest wall at the end of the narrow room to be just one large mouth—slightly open and faintly breathing in and out. I just stood there and stared, astounded, feeling the slight breath on me. Finally I just let out a scream, crying out at the enormity of it all. I looked around. The rest of the narrow room was empty. There was nothing left to do, so I knelt down and crawled back through that little door. I was beaten down by the hugeness of it all, drained and tired. I curled up on the small kitchen floor, the hard linoleum feeling harder than it should, the small door mocking me with its unbelievable smallness, its uselessness. I curled up and wept at the smallness of it all. And now I wonder if it was really all a dream or not, afraid to actually look under my sink)

I passed an empty lot filled with old tires, refrigerators, washing machines, couches, a burnt-out car, a toilet, a sink, a bed frame, a grocery cart, and the like. Several children were playing in the old car. For some reason one of them had an old paper grocery bag on his head and was just sitting quietly in the back seat as if just waiting for something to happen, as if the kid lived in that empty lot and was just comfortable being home, or maybe he was waiting for that car to start up and take him somewhere more magical than anywhere he knew.

(feeling #127—Those kids are so lucky, they're mostly unspoiled by life, not burdened by their dreams, haven't made too many mistakes, haven't had too many lies told about them or to them yet. I guess regrets are an indication you've lived a big life with lots of choices, it's just that I see all these people out and about with girlfriends and boyfriends and I marvel at how they managed to get that to happen. It's like the Gods of Love prefer them more than they love me. Or maybe it's just that I'm too preoccupied with stupid matters that don't really matter. Or maybe it's just that I'm too prideful, never was smart enough to say "Please don't go." Yeah, I guess it's always in the things you didn't try that end up making a difference. But for now, for today, maybe I'll be able to get some stuff cleaned up. Maybe I could at least do that much)

I passed an old brick church, out of which poured a series of children as if a blur of ghosts racing into the future. They seemed to be shooting at one another in a "cops-and-robbers" kind of way as opposed to a "playing war" kind of way. They flowed around the side, past an old light blue pickup truck with a gun rack and a small American flag sticker in the corner of the back window, and into the back parking lot.

(feeling #128—I always thought it strange that many religious people were also very enthusiastic about shooting things, killing animals, and supportive of conquering other people and other lands, about taming the perceived wild, about instilling their template down on you, and hostile to anyone who didn't support our country's wars with all their hearts. I thought it odd that many people who are religious also play shoot 'em up video games and love action movies where tons of dudes get blasted, dig wrestling and football and other activities that glorify defeating someone—that many of these movies had a simple and singular construct: that it was OK for you to kill the

bad guy if he harmed someone close to you. But wouldn't the religion they support hold them to a higher moral standard?)

I got to the library and went straight for the "President" section. I wanted to check President Lincoln out, but he had been checked out already, so I had to settle for President John F. Kennedy. (Over the years they had perfected the Clones. At first they started with synthetic robots, but they were a little stiff. The organic Clones are looser and much more realistic. But what they didn't know was that instead of using them to learn about history, or how to resolve conflicts peacefully and fairly, or to listen to a Jimi Hendrix play "Little Wing" or a Chet Baker play "My Funny Valentine", I was using the Clones to do the dishes, vacuuming, laundry, lawn mowing, gutter cleaning, painting, and what-all. I can only assume others were pulling the same scam).

(thought #85—I guess when they started with the Clones they thought if everyone had their own private maid and butler and handyman, that would be considered "lazy" on our part, maybe people would become complacent and our society would stagnate and regress. Or that it was hinting that it was somehow "acceptable" to "own" someone else, own their thoughts and control them somehow, limit their freedoms. So it was considered bad form to have a Clone of your own. People who would be found hiding one would be fined and reported on the news. It was very embarrassing and would cost you friends. Now there are special locks and programmed limits to the Instructor Clones. Clones do not obey certain requests. They are programmed to just do their thing, just the history part, the acting it all out, just be who they are, do what they know. But you never know. I'm sure there are people out there who find a way. For example, I have a crack for all that. I can break in and turn that all off. I can program them and make them eager to please. I assume others have such ability too. And, really, who knows—maybe Ekborg or Emberg are really just Clones. Maybe you or I are just a Clone, someone else's puppet, programmed to do someone else's bidding)

Yeah, the Clones come in handy. I'll get Kennedy home

and started in on helping out around the place—on that dining room, on the sorting, on clearing out all the clutter. We dare to do these things, and all the other things, not because they are easy, but because they are hard. You wouldn't believe how things pile up. Maybe he'll also have time to get started on the bathroom before I have to return him. Yeah, sometimes it's nice to get things cleaned up, cleared out, get things done. Other times it's just nice to have someone else around.

gusts in the alleys

the idiot's guide to morons

(dave granger is in grave danger)

dave-o and me at work

me and dave granger work in the back of the bottling plant on the east side. It's a really nice job—everyone leaves us alone, the work isn't too bad—and best of all, we can drink all we want and walk out with an armload under our jackets whenever we please. it's a sweet gig

now if you ever actually met me, you'd probably not peg me as a loser right off because I dress well—I don't sport expensive or elaborate clothing (I wouldn't be able to afford brand new or fancy tailored duds), I get my clothes second hand at vintage and charity clothing places, and I can assure you I dress with a crisp taste and style—optimistic, with an assured authority—beyond that I'm probably a loser (and probably dave too) because nothing ever seems to work in my favor, I don't try real hard, because why even bother, I take my own sweet time, because where is there to be, I don't need any of that fancy big city talk, because why be impressed by any of that phony crap, and sure we ain't got nothing to do, I'm not clever enough to figure it all out, my friends are probably losers too, of course they're morons and I'm tired of them and they're tired of me, but at least I ain't got nothin' ta lose—now, pass the bottle opener an' get back ta work

yeah, you probably wouldn't dig me, but at least I got

style, an' that's worth a lot—it ain't something you can just buy or learn, it's innate, and davey-boy and the others have a style and knowledge all their own too—it wasn't bought out of a catalog or preformulated on a TV show

so, let's ogle us some women

so we end up at the bowling alley with dave's cousins, and for some reason we're all being kind of defensive in that we're just hanging out way at the end and just staying away from people in general because they're always hasslin' us for no good reason, an' at the moment we just ain't in the mood, but dave, oh davey boy, he's constantly trying to talk to these gals a few lanes over, but they're not interested and keep shooting him down, but he's persistent—like those smooth guys on television, but after a while they just end up ignoring him completely, so he starts in on another group of gallies and they just end up yelling at him, and eventually it gets to the point where me and his cousins are laughing our asses off as it slips into this pathetic, absurd routine—I mean here dave's got like a 220 game hanging and he just keeps drifting off to talk to some gals, only not one of 'em is really interested so he always ends up back here with us at his turn because who wants to hold up the game?

oh, and he's wearing a white t-shirt that he has written on in big, crude letters: "free hugs"

good plan

we just sit and watch, talking about the ball game on up in the corner behind us and about work and fishing in the link between the reservoir and the lake at the park, and trying to get dave-o to idle down a few notches, but then after a while of watching dave-o it starts to get fascinating, like what's the point? what's the point of even trying?

but you know, as it gets towards the end, we're almost rooting for him, he actually seems like he's getting close to getting a phone number or something a couple of times here, and all that tragic bowling alley rejection and late night failure just doesn't seem to faze him, I mean it gets to the end of the evening here and we just can't believe it—like he's worked his ass off all week just to end up here—I mean it's so brutal watching it all unfold after a while, him making the rounds, working the room, heaps of rejection piled on him, like what's the point even? and I mean all night long—like four hours worth, an ample portion—here he's being a gentleman—calm and polite all night, but just getting nowhere, and we're all just laughin' at 'im and suggesting he just stick with us for a while and not bother people as maybe it's just not his night, and after a while we even stop apologizing to people for him, but you know, it's Friday night and he's just so keyed up an' all, like he's been waiting to get out all week, and he just shrugs: "how do you think people meet?" which is a valid stance, I guess, it just doesn't really seem to be his crowd in here tonight, that's all—if you know what I mean, I mean he isn't in the flow or hittin' smooth or ridin' that mysterious current of night or rockin' the boogie, so why bother, ya know? but he still keeps on keepin' on, approaching the unapproachable—strange girls, exotic bowling alley women, dark shadowy ladies—and keeps getting turned away, and you know, when we're leaving, re-submerging into that back alley existence of ours, the only place in this world that will leave us be, returning to that oily, oil-stained shadowland, I open my mouth and say something really profound like, "nice job, dorkus," and just as we step from the blinding white void of bowling alley, plunging into that waterfall of night, dave looks over to me and goes, "oh yeah, well at least I talked to some girls tonight, some actual girls— I mean, what did you do? you just sat there," to which I reply, "but you didn't even talk to any of them, they didn't want to talk to you, they didn't even bother with you, they dismissed you outright, they didn't want anything to do with you, smoothie, they all told you to basically get lost, you're bothering us, we want to be left alone, even in that polite nice girl way of theirs of letting you know that they're busy," and dave shrugs, and just goes, "well, I talked to 'em," and I mean, the pride in his voice suddenly becomes the only thing in that cavernous darkness, that feeling of accomplishment, that he actually did something, tried something, that it startles me, to the point that I am actually taken aback for a moment, like all night I'm thinkin' this guy just doesn't have it, that he's a real no-talent loser, a lifeless anemic washout, I mean, maybe dave-o is right, at least he *talked* to some girls, at least he *tried*, "I mean, what happens in the future?" he counters, continuing, "if I ever run into any of 'em? Now I have an opening, I can say 'hey, remember when we met bowling? remember when we talked, but you were kinda busy with your friends...' I mean, you gotta pretend you're already friends, convince 'em they already know you, they trust you, you're harmless, they'll have a righteous time with you. I mean, you gotta have an opening, man, an 'in'—that's the hardest part, that's your golden ticket. So I got that to put in my back pocket and carry around with me for the rest of my life—all those openings, all those golden tickets..." and just then a big ol' sedan rumbles past in the dust and darkness of the alley, and some big guys chuck beer bottles at us and we have to duck and scatter until that unmistakable "clunk, clunk, clunk" of empty beer bottles slamming projectile-like into dumpsters and brick walls and the asphalt and brick of the alley floor, and then that one unmistakable, hollow "clunk" of empty beer bottle against noggin rings out in the dark night and we hear dave drop with a wet thump against the hard ground to splay out on the cracked and oil-stained pavement and we run over and feel him there in the darkness, even though it's too dark to see as he rolls around holding his throbbing noggin and moaning, so I rush up and to make him feel better I just stand above him as he rolls back and forth mumbling and moaning and holding his noodle and I just say, "man, yer mom's an ugly whore" and just as I figure, dave pops to his feet and springs after me, lunging in the darkness—I spin away and he gives chase and we're running and running like invisible winds in the oily darkness and I hear him behind me, huffing, gaining, groaning, gasping, so I stagger up to a spot where I know a telephone pole is (I grew up in these alleys, playing kickball and hide-and-seek while waiting for mom to return from the bar, while hiding from the rich kids who would tease me, while trying to escape that closet of an apartment me and mom had to share) and just as he gets to me I spin away and he slams smack into the side of the pole with a slapping wet "thwap" in the dark gritty night and we all just break up like it's the funniest thing we've seen in hours, as dave-o staggers about then drops in the dust, so I hustle over as he sort of groans and moves real slow, trying to get up, so I unzip, ready to cut a whiz all over him, and that really gets him going, lunging at me, trying to drag me down, so I start in again with the whole "ya didn't talk to 'em," and he's all "but I did," and I'm nothing but "what did you even talk about? huh? what a pest you're being? ... that's not even close to a proper conversation, not even in the same neighborhood," which sends him lunging after me, which I expected, so I spin away at the last split second and dave-o whaps into that same back-alley telephone pole again

and what do you know, the guy doesn't even go down this time, he just sort of sidesteps and staggers a few feet in a circle and then starts in on me, "so I talked to some girls tonight and you didn't, you're just jealous and resentful," and I reply with "but you *didn't* talk to them—they didn't even want to talk to you—sitting down and having a beer and some actual in-depth conversation is what *'talking to girls'* is all about," so he counters with, "yeah, well what if one of 'em ended up talking to me? huh? one of 'em might've—an' maybe I'd get her number and we could go out? maybe have a nice, gentle time of it, nothing like the rattling and heat at work, huh? how do I know which one would talk to me or not? I don't know one from the other, I don't know which one, so I guess I have to talk to 'em all to find out, huh? what then? what if one of 'em is nice, maybe even starts ta like me? huh? what then genius? how will I know which ones to talk to or not unless I approach them?" "but you were bothering them—*bothering* them—an', man, take it from me—girls don't like to be bothered," "so I need to make a few subtle adjustments in my delivery, that's all, just some minor refinements, then you'll see, eventually if I keep tryin', eventually it just might happen, I might just hit smooth, you'll see, an' where will you be during all this? huh? sittin' over there off to the side, partially in the darkness like always, while I'll be in the glorious glowing brightness of some gal's bright smile to light my way... I mean, when you sit back and watch, sometimes life just doesn't happen the way you'd expect—this way, at least maybe I might have a little hand in my own destiny—yeah, eventually the odds are in my favor—eventually it's bound to happen for me, I'll improve, I can feel it out there stirring in that darkness, in the emptiness, in the weeds, in the garbage, in the gusts, out beyond that great beyond, just waiting for me to find it in that stew ... that's what I figure ... with enough practice, eventually I'm bound to get good at talkin' to girls, experimenting and probing until I find out just what they like, you'll see ... I mean, what other options do I have? and most importantly, what if ... what if one day one of 'em actually says yes? what then? huh? how 'bout that?"

(I have to admit, it almost makes sense—all that hoping, but then love always made me behave stupidly, so I wonder what the hope for love could do to someone like dave—someone who's always in love with the thought of being in love, I mean, how would that make a person feel and behave? that always chasing after something elusive, that always expecting things to happen, that always grasping at the wind and passing fog, that always hoping, I mean, if you had that weighing on you all the time, if you were infected with those feelings, if you were always relegated to the sidelines, if you were always left there waiting, if you were a loser, wouldn't you want to do something about it eventually too? wouldn't you end up trying just about anything and everything to relieve yourself of those feelings? ... and I tell you, I'm not jealous of him, I'm just tired, I just didn't want to get kicked out of that bowling alley again—it's one of the few places to go around here, a place you can go when you have no other place to go—in fact, I think I might actually admire his courage, the fact that he can still keep hoping. I didn't have the heart to tell him that there was no secret, that all the women were different, that there was no single key to it all, no magic word that worked to open it all up)

amidst the hootings and yee-haws

I remember telling dave in that bowling palace, amidst the revelry, hootings, and yee-haws of the people beyond us, that I wasn't up for it just then—that whole "approaching-strange-girls" thing—it was all just too much work. I guess I'm just burnt out on all that, and I didn't see the point in wasting the energy, letting your hopes get up only to be disappointed—but what I didn't tell him is that, in reality, I am merely a brute wandering a fragile world and bumping into things in the most inelegant of manners—that any girl I would happen upon would be too fragile for me and that I would surely soon soil or crush whatever desperate, single chance I would ever even hope to have with her in the first place with whatever clumsy, awkward words I could somehow come up with, and that yes, even though I am an accidental brute, trapped in a fragile world, I really don't mind it all that much anymore, I mean, you are who you are after a while, an' besides, I have a nice piece of chocolate cake and a new copy of "the best of mountain" waiting for me at home—it's just the uselessness of words and feelings that gets to me some-times—the fact that they were meant for other people and not for me—that's the sad, frustrating part—that words get crushed when they finally fumble around and escape from my mouth—meanings become distorted, stretched, mangled, crumpled, and how too much always comes out all at once, as if everything inside, everything I've ever seen or heard, everything I've ever wanted to express or share with someone else all wants to come out all at once, that it all wants to escape from me if only given the chance

a mountain of wind holding us back

(then something caught my eye—just a flash in the window of a car turning a corner up ahead—just a blink of a girl I used to know back when things were easier, back when I was somebody, back when I had it all, all the comfort and security of another, back when I had all the answers, now faded to old questions, rusted in place, back when I had her, when I had something permanent, something to look forward to, back when I had her, when I knew everything, when everything came together and fell into place, when everything was so much smoother and more dependable, before it all disappeared around unseen corners, from a life so condensed, so concentrated into a bright focus—and now I'm burned out, waiting for someone or something to re-ignite me, other blurry lights in the unfocused distance now burning brighter and bigger than me, as girls pass invisibly at a rate I can't seem to catch up to, passing on winds of sharp flashes and quick glimpses of what I once had, all I could've been, reduced now to only quick sparks that flash out before I can even realize what was there—until all that is left is just me, standing alone in an alley in the darkness with the other randomly displaced—scattered, and unseen. just a flash, as always: a girl I used to know, trapped in a car turning a corner, then obscured by huge unmovable objects—sagging buildings and old darkness and time)

a flash of a girl in a rush of dark colors from a speeding car—a girl I used to know until she just disappeared one day in a rushing blur and now that's all I know of her, just those brief glimpses, just that smear of blur and sparks and flashes of winds. and in thinking of her it just gets me in such a foul mood, remembering all I could've had, all I've been missing out on—and as I think and stew on this, I just start calmly informing the gray blobs of strangers who pass in the night, "man, yer mom's an ugly whore," shaking my head in shame and looking down in pity for added effect and really laying it on with a granite-like indifference to the point that every once in a while one of 'em really becomes offended and tries to chase me, but luckily one of my fellow advocates usually sticks his foot out and sends them into the hard dusty ground which generally cools them out awhile as I continue to refer to people as "ugly whores" for no real reason other than it's just a sad thing to have your life reduced to flashes of colors that dissipate and shrink so fast you can't even take a step to try an' catch up

that and the fact that it's getting late and I guess I just want to get them thinking on another plane, whether they are in fact ugly, or whores, or either, or both, but hey, they want to fight, and if there's one thing I've learned over the years is we all have to fight something I guess, I know *that*, at least, and I guess I've figured out a couple of other things along the way here too, more things than I'd care to admit—like beauty comes from *need*, and that life springs from emotion, raw feelings, and I also think I know God in a way I hope you never will—the taking God—the taking taking taking and leaving only empty, windy, dirty, expanses of nothing as far as the eye can see, and in thinking of this and that brief blur that reminds me of what we had, what we could've been so that for the rest of the night everything else seems so spoiled and rotten and left behind like an ugly whore—a dark windy humaneless void that I want to lash out at and tear into for making me feel so lousy and empty and forgotten—that time has slowed down for me and I miss the blur of it all, the rush of belonging to that swirl, of not always having to sit and wait from the sidelines, waiting my entire life, of not participating, of not rushing with the current, but always watching from a distance, from a dark, dirty corner, of always waiting

and then I see at the end of the alley, bobbing in that little puddle of streetlight at the tip of that barrel of darkness, the outlet of the venice-like channels of our back alley world, the outlet to the great mysteries beyond, finally, at the end of it all, there in that speck of light, that flickering end-of-it-all-ness—is dave being swung around in the air by his collar, so I call out to the others and we all rush down, fighting the heavy wind, to find some big guys from the bowling alley hasslin' dave-o—and I feel so bad for him now, swinging by the thick meat hooks of some big guy, as if hanging by the fists of time itself, some big shadow raising dave into the night by his best friday night finery, the wind trying its best to hold us back, trying its best to keep us down and out as usual, and as I race up the sandy alley I swipe the lid off a garbage can, and the night is flowing right through me, and I become the night, the darkness, the breeze ... and the alleys grow to stretch on before us like strings drained of their color, the alleys stretching on

as we rush up the alley, tommy reaches low for a handful of sand, jimmy scoops up a bottle, haymer removes his belt and begins swinging it ritualistically, as if we're a machine roaring into action and I see the guy lets dave drop with a thump and by the time we get there the big guys are gone, disappearing like cowards, and dave is on the ground, sitting up, brushing himself off—"what was that all about?" someone behind me asks as we search the blankness for more baddies—"was talkin' to some of their gals," dave climbs to his feet and looks around—"their girlfriends?" "no, just some gals who was with 'em ... just some peeps from their crowd ... they don't like no outsiders 'round here much, not 'round in these parts none anyway, hey"

they were some guys whose gals dave was tryin' to get to know—an' that just really upsets my apple cart—that these

guys were hassling' him just 'cause he wanted to talk to someone, someone new—just wanted some warm soft company,
some fresh new company (as opposed to us tired, boresome
losers with apparently nothing better to do than pick away at
one another, with nothing better to do than get beat on by
life), just because all he wants is someone gentle to talk to,
some real nice gal to look deep into his eyes and maybe whisper his name back to him, maybe whisper his name into that
deep empty void of night, filling it all with her breath—that's
all, that's all he wants, all he feels he really needs out of this
flat, blank, deflated existence—all he really needs—to be
inflated by another's breath, to breathe life into his day, bring
color and a fresh perspective—so it really really really got
under my skin and good when I saw him in that faint little
pinprick of a spotlight down there, 'cause it felt like I was sort
of looking at myself somehow, that I was the pinprick, the
tiny glow in the great expanse

a return to the warm, fuzzy abyss

as we turn back into the night, back into our backwater
abyss of narrow back alley sand and inside-out world of stacks
of old tires and pallets and dumpsters and used-up appliances
in tall grass and nothingness, back into our kingdom of stains,
cracks, weeds, banished items and wrung-out yester things,
back into our own hidden cocoon, old used-up days faded,
rusted, crumpled, frayed, stacked and hidden away, into the
place no one ever really knows, back into the in-between
space, back into feelings you'll never admit, feelings someone
like you will never know, feelings you hand down to us with
your contempt, back into our forgotten back-world sanctuary
of warm, comfortable, furry darkness all our own that nobody
else wants or even knows about, that no one else can ever
attempt to spoil, we all try our best to reassure dave—"they
just couldn't handle your daveness, that's all—the magnitude
of your massive dudeishness, the divine daveitude of your

deity, your density, your sheer mass, your velocity—it's on a totally other plane man, a level they can't decipher, a frequency so advanced, so beyond them they can't reach or translate."—"your coolness needs to be contained in concrete bunkers deep in the desert, like nuclear waste, that's all, we should pity them their limited viewpoint, their primitive minds, for they cannot foresee your higher-level comprehension, your destiny is beyond their measure, beyond their reach, and they're just starting to glimpse that—it's that simple"—"they're just intimidated by your beautiful freedom, your lightness, your gravitational pull, your gravity"—"yeah, man, they're so terrified by your beautiful freedom it triggers a territorial aggression in them, a fear-aggression of the less-evolved, that's all"—"yeah, man, I pity their plant-life brains, their plankton-like simplicity, the fact they can't tune in to your various frequencies"—"yeah, they're just so insecure about you, that's all—they know people like you reduce them to gossipy gutless cowards—I mean, that's really all they have when you get down to it—just do the math, distill it down, and that's all that's really there—their gossip and desperation, their elbowing people out of the way, their keeping people down, their expecting things to just be handed to them instead of earning things on their own merit—I mean, really, besides being mean to people and being terrified cowards, what've they ever done?"—"Yeah man, they can't reach you, that's all, can't find that range to tune in to you, you're just too far beyond them, more advanced, deeper"—"you are a bright shining prince among enfeebled dung beetles, and I am inspired by your glow, it lights my way through the darkness, through the doubt"

when walking back we pass stacks of garbage, but some of it is not garbage, some just good stuff some people just aren't using right now—bikes, chairs, filing cabinet, a bench, a desk, a lamp, a set of shelves—man, you wouldn't believe the stuff people throw away, new stuff, good stuff—it would break your heart—it's like they just can't help themselves, just don't see the goodness, just don't know any better, just can't see

and in thinking of this I reconsider a few things, I mean, like sure, I know I'm a loser, and a professional loser at that, with years of experience of nothing working out—dismissed from school, the army, jobs, apartments, groups of friends, girlfriends, potential girlfriends, left behind—why even pretend anymore? does it even matter at this point? but at least I'm not out causing too much trouble—at least I'm not out hurting people, I'm not one of those cowardly creeps pretending to be something I'll never be, at least I'm not some poser, some fast talker always trying to sell myself, impress people, put others down all the time—I mean I am what I am and I'm content with that and nothing and no one's going to change that—I found a groove, and people who bring out something no one else could, and in them I find the better parts of myself, so, no, I'm not one of those cowardly creeps clinging to some pathetic worn-out clique or pose handed to them from someone else, at least I can think for myself (at least I want what I have and am not shoving it in people's faces, at least I know enough to start my own crowd, have my own thoughts—I mean, if you don't like what's on television, start your own show, don't like the stories you're hearing—start your own stories, don't like the clubs around you—start your own clubs, not getting invited to the parties—start your own parties)

it's just the randomness of it all that's starting to bother me

the darkness is peaceful, it gets me to thinking that I really should stop dave, save him from that sting of rejection that never leaves. he'll say I'm jealous, but I should see beyond that contention, but then I think on it some more and reconsider—maybe that pain helps the grass grow, propels the clouds, makes them churn and ooze, helps the wind cool you out, activates all the free beauty, inflates it all, fills it all with color, all the ornament, but then maybe there are even more options to consider beyond just those two

a shadow appears in the shadows, we can perceive them because of all our time spent in the shadows, we know one from another, we can separate that which is flat and pressed down, mooshed together, we can inflate the shadows—it's just some random dude relieving himself, who turns when he perceives our scuffle, our breathing—he is startled, too many against one, "oh, hey, it's you," he nods, turning and zipping up as a small grey light in the distance tries to define us, tries to bring us into relief, "it's you, my man," he gestures lazily to dave-o, quickly taking note of our measure, "you that smooth operator, my man, yeah, I seen you in there tonight, wish I was smooth like you, could work the room, make all those flash connections, in the mix, getting to know"

"ya gotta get out there, reveal you're a person of substance," dave nods as we pass, "you have a good night"

"will do what I can," the shadow turns to dissipate, mixing into all the other darkness

shadows can be nice, a quiet place no one can bother you, an accomplishment if you can figure out how to blend in, but they can also be a trap, a cage, limiting your progress, and if you can find a way to turn that dichotomy on and off, then you've really mastered something

it got me to thinking, the dark figure we just passed could be a version of us from earlier in our lives, or maybe a possibility of what we will become, but when we were younger, we were going to inflate the world, give it color and depth, but then we got too tired, worked too much, dissipated our energy, and then the world chased us away

it's the big schweez, man

as we walk back down the alley, through that thin watery

darkness, someone in that distant darkness calls out "losers" and "freaks" in our direction, and even though they're aimed at us from cowards hiding in that darkness, we all just continue on like it's nothing—we don't chase after, they're just words shot at us to try to pierce our comfortable world of silence, to keep us down, elbow us out of the way, hold us in place, try to define us, but we know all that crap is just to try to divert us, waste our time, bog us down, and that's a big schweez if there ever was one, man—trying to divert someone and bog them down with your insecurities—and man, sometimes it just feels like it's coming from just about everywhere—every mouth, every advertisement—we know it isn't true, so why bother with it, yet we also know that, in a sense, it is true—I mean, should we be out there doing more? trying more? sure, we're hanging out in the inside fold, in the unseen grooves, in the shadows, with nothing to lose, nothing to try for, hiding in an insular, comfortable sameness—I guess we could be visiting the sick and imprisoned, helping the elderly and disadvantaged, cleaning up the park, but I can't see those situations being any different than anything else out there—those places are also populated with people tryin' to schweez you at every turn, man—schweez you out of the way and down to nothing, take it all from you, hog it all for themselves, trying to turn you into something you're not—something they need you to be so they can feel better about their crappy do-nothing lives, or into something they want you to be—a puppet, a pet monkey, a loser, someone without faith or hope, they want to use you to make themselves look better, they want to take it all away from you, leave you with nothing, they want it all for themselves

and you know, I almost recognize that voice, as if that voice were a ghost that knows me, but then all those deep empty night voices think they know me, think they're better than everyone else, think they know everything, think they know the unknowable, to the point that sometimes I almost feel as if I'm on the other end of those voices, calling out to strangers, to ghosts, as if at one time I were the one hoping to keep people down, trying to keep people in place, trying to label it all, take it all, as if those frozen invisible words are now only an echo from out of my past, sent back for revenge, keeping people from getting to know me, as if I were calling out to myself, trying to keep myself down—it all gets me to thinking—I don't want to be that person anymore, I don't want to be that guy, I don't ever want to hurt anyone else ever again, I've seen way too much of that for one lifetime, I've seen way too many bad things ... me, I just want to be left alone ... and that's another big schweez, man—you can add that one to the list too

even 4 out of 5 idiots know that

am I really a loser? am I really that bad? huh? should I just give up like this? give up trying, just slump down to hide in the safety of the shadows, in the creases? hiding out at home, never going out, never meeting anyone new? am I the only one who's ever felt this way, is a person really ever useless, is it all about practice, or luck, or just all that there is, all that you get?

or maybe I should just enter that other plane of existence like johnny over there and just pretend I'm somewhere else, or maybe I should just get cookin'—maybe it all just rests on hard work, hard work just for its own sake, just for a challenge, just to see if I can do it, I mean, that must be it, huh? I mean, even four out of five idiots must know at least that much

and I get to looking around sometimes, wondering if other people have better lives than mine, have it easier, wondering why other people are luckier than me? (and not fancy desperate poser cars or insecure artifice, but depth, meaning, knowledge, weight) wondering if I just wanted too much? wondering: did I have a good life? could've I tried harder?

lets ruin the planet for everyone (let's pave the world with our indifference)

every so often I wonder if I could really blame them for yelling things into the night, what with how tough, uncaring, and indifferent the world can be at times what with all the struggles, frustration, obstacles—the clutch fading out, doesn't stick tight no more, the garage door opener grinding the plastic to nothing, the lawn mower rusting through and not starting, the tape player in the car whirling but not catching and then slowing to a drone, the house settling in a bad lean so the back door won't even open, Janet the girl I liked moving so far away it felt as though that distance was stretching me out so thin there wouldn't be any room left for anyone else to live inside me anymore, so thin it made me not want to know anyone anymore

but then you realize that even in the back alleys you can't be free of all the feelings you haven't even had time to identify and name yet

and then there's such a thing as maybe holding on too tightly

standing here in the dark and thinking about all of this—I guess now maybe I'm starting to see dave granger in a little different light, or maybe he's still really the same person he always was, I just never got to see this side of him or realize he was more deep or three dimensional—but maybe that was all on me, me keeping him down, me only seeing what I wanted to see, me only seeing him for what I wanted or needed him to be, and now I view him as an explorer of the human heart, but as with all explorers I fear what's going to happen is he will get out there too far, too far away from everything he knows and into that dangerous wilderness—and I don't mean that in a cynical way, I just don't think he's going to find anything out there, nothing like he knows here with us that is—like a lot of explorers of the human condition—he'll get too far out there and there won't be anything or anyone else around and he'll get lonely and miss us—so I just think he's better off by hanging back a little and letting life come to him—but I guess he's a man of action, not one to sit and wait for things to find him—and maybe I'm just afraid of losing him, that if he does end up with a girl, she'll just whisk him away on her wind, and then what'll I be left with? just a small apartment with nothing but a table full of bills waiting for me at the end of the day

an' man, I'm sure tired of people disappearing, tired of the constant change, that everything is bound to slip away

and I think of more fears I have for him, and want to protect him from them, want to wrap him in bubble wrap and put him up on a high shelf and keep him safe forever—I'm afraid he'll end up getting hurt, growing jaded, end up like me, all closed off, empty, with nothing left to share, nowhere else to go, fearing he'll meet some of the negative women, the devil's cousin, dust's daughter, rust's niece—so please dave, don't ever develop an argumentative nature—please be agreeable, please be on time, remain sober-minded, good natured, supportive, attentive, willing to please, well-groomed, financially solvent, helpful but not a doormat, charitable but not to the wrong folk, generous with your time, money and affections—please remember to be well organized, tidy, chipper, full of pep, keep your chin up, get plenty of rest, eat healthy, take a walk, don't worry, speak well of others lest something comes back on you, use good judgment, practice good hygiene, be optimistic, always smile like the village fool, be reliable and positive, compliment others like your life depends on it, think for yourself, and let all the good things descend upon you like a plague of locusts and dave, oh dave, please, please do not forget to wear the colors of the day, lest ye risk ridicule and banishment—I mean really, please dave, please, stay current in your fashions, please keep watch of the trends, you would not want to fall so far behind

I've noticed dave has been sleeping through entire days lately, and I'm concerned—or maybe dave-o just knows something that most of us others don't—that it's all just a state of mind, that it's all just a big schweez

and then dave's about to get that look on his face, when he drifts off to the side, just barely hanging on the fringes, wearin' those tight tight tight artsy red pants, doing what he calls his "crazy eyes" dance—just stiffly shuffling along and kind of twitching a tight, shivering jiggle and staring with huge saucer eyes, shivering in a shaking shimmy, a trance dance that I always enjoyed and appreciated, as if he were dancing just to amuse the likes of me, his eternal silent shake, his forever stare, as if in deep concentration, tunneling deep into himself, mining the soul, a soul miner, shaking and staring as if shaking out his demons, as if shaking free of arbitrary customs and norms, as if shaking loose from what constrains him

(and I don't just care desperately about dave because he's my friend or because it's the right thing to do, or because he's a "guy" and thus in caring about him I would somehow be caring about myself in a somewhat selfish way or that I would be caring about the entirety of humanity as a whole in a non-selfish manner—no, I mean I really don't want to see dave get hurt because we were housemates once living in the same house with the same people and pressures and dramas and events for over two and a half oh my lordy years a few years ago, and sure, even though we are very different people, he is still my friend and I guess I don't want to see him stick his neck out and get hurt in any of the various ways, traditional and nontraditional, some of them mentioned and evidenced above, but it is even more deep than that about how in a way living so close together like that it was like eventually he sort of absorbed me and me him in that transparent living-together way, him getting to know just about all my habits and secrets—and in a sense I know most of his habits and secrets too, and most of our secrets were and probably are basically fairly similar and so it is as if he is somehow a carrier (a holder, if you will) of most if not all of my secrets, and in that way I want to keep him safe—as if to keep my secrets safe and contained so they don't spill or float off to who knows where, possibly getting trampled, lost, ruined, or at the very least soiled with filth of who knows what kind—all of my disappointments and embarrassments—all of my mistakes and flaws, even the one's I've purposely forgotten about (and those forgotten mistakes have seemed to forever fuse us together in an invisible link)—all of my silly, fragile hopes and desperate dreams, silly and/or unimpressive as they may be—and even though I know I should probably get over myself and not be so protective and self-preserving and let all my dreams go with the wind so I can grow some fresh new ones, so I can maybe somehow possibly someday move on, I mean the past is in the past after all—past mistakes, past embarrassments, but somehow I still hold them all way way way too close, thinking of them as real and alive, with no expiration dates, so they don't run right through my arms, but alas, events are so perishable and people tend to get busy and forget and why oh why can't I let them go? ... why can't I just let her go? ... and in a way dave is a container to hold them, and I wouldn't want to lose that container or see it breached)

the gusts in the alleys

jimmy spilt some garbage from one of the greasy bars and was now lining up the chicken bones in the back alley sand (jimmy was always surly, today because he had switched bar-bers. it's tough. his main friend killer joe was in the can for speeding, even though he had no place to go, no place to be, so was at this point unavailable. they called him killer joe because he looked like your average joe, which was certainly a clever disguise, a "put on", his real name is stanley, and because he had bad luck with animals—all his pets ended up not living very long, or just giving up and running away), "come on," I implore, but he's down on all fours, shaking his head, "not done, not done yet," while dave straddles the dark-ness, shivering a stiff, tight shimmy, head shaking, body twitching to some new wave song in his head, staring into the abyss, as spencer chucks bottles randomly into the darkness, as if to fight off the randomness of it all with a little random-ness of his own, his own protest against the randomness, the only thing he has to announce his displeasure, the only thing he has to fight back against the randomness, while delbert whispers encouragements, and not to be out done, Jai is scratching in the dirt with a stick, "whatcha drawin'?" I ven-ture, "vaginas" he chuckles, "some serious business, eh?" I offer, "if you say so," he shrugs, and as I wander down to him I notice that sure enough he has scratched out about a dozen in a row, each about two feet long, though it is clear he is inexpe-rienced in this venture, his knowledge of the technique and subject quite limited at this time

(eventually they hauled jimmy away, somehow they found out he was some type of spy from some far away place—he was spying on us at work, the people who sent him thought our bottling plant might really be a secret lab, though I never saw anything secret in there, and even though to the best of our knowledge we're not secret lab people, we all found the fact jimmy thought we might be to be really cute

they think Jai fell into the link between the reservoir and the lake at the park one night, in any case he was never seen again, the night whisking him away while drinking too much and now we will never be blessed with that sly smile again, with his quick belt, his quiet proficiency with the garbage can lid. spencer got another job on the north side of the east side and ended up hanging out with people he met up there, and we barely saw him anymore, leaving us with just glimpses, just flashes

eventually delbert ran out of options, he got laid off from the plant, and then they took everything away from him, so he joined the military where they told him he was righteous, heroic, though we could've told him that, and the president sent him to die in a cold hard field of stones as far away from anything he'd ever known so the president's golfing buddies could make even more money, but it was OK, they said, because they told him and his family that he was a hero, but we knew that only cowards talked like that, only people who didn't know what it was like in those situations, so he died a fool, a chump, he was blown apart so badly that none of those stones would remember him in their thoughts, none of the presidents would whisper his name into the night, their breath not calming, not able to reach his mother, and I think about all that every now and then and I add it all up and realize that I don't need any of those false, dishonest, fleeting victories, I don't want the temporary glory other people who don't know me try to convince me I should want, I don't care about winning or any of that rotting sick money, I just want him back here with me, whispering encouragements ... that would be victory enough, that would be all his mother could hope to ask for

it was the same in high school—the coach telling him he was a hero as he ran as fast as the wind into the other team on a kickoff, messing his back up so bad he never walked right again—it was the same thing as always

as for me, I guess I just want a future, I just don't want to wait around forever, wasting time here in the past, time that I could use to make something new)

maybe I should just let dave go and do what he feels he must, but dave's potential demise would project negatively on me, so why can't I seem to let dave go, let him be? either way I want to protect him, and all our secrets there within, for he is still a vessel of my feelings, he is, in a sense, an extension of myself because he is in my world, close to me (oh the horrible chafing closeness), a full-time member of my life, for the time being at least, and thus my experiences are his experiences, and his experiences are mine and thus must be looked after in some way, right? (of course I should be talking—you know, like I should even be considering telling him, or anyone else for that matter, what he should be doing—compared to his, my love life is as scenic as the inside of a moldy cinderblock pump house) but I should just let him go, I've decided, so he can grow and move forward—just one more thing for me to lose in life, just one more change, just one more thing to slip away

but I'm afraid of losing dave, of losing all that is familiar and comfortable, of all I know changing on me, of myself changing, of maybe losing the best parts of myself, and if dave changes, so will the rest of my life accelerate in a domino pattern—yeah, I'm so afraid of dave changing, of him moving away from me, because that would mean that I would have to change, and even now I can feel him moving ever so slightly away from the rest of us—I'm afraid of dave changing, and I'm afraid of dave not changing and evolving, and I'm afraid of keeping him from changing, and I'm afraid that I will push him too hard to be something he doesn't want or isn't ready for, and I'm afraid of ruining the friendship and losing dave and all that is contained within—the comfort and familiarity—and I guess what I might really fear is losing myself—of changing too much or not at all, and that I'm merely using dave as a gauge to judge myself, using him only as a mirror instead of appreciating him for his unique and special shining daveness—and that seems to be one of the weird things: that delicate expiration date, or maybe I'm looking down on him for "falling behind" or something, and you know I want dave to still be my friend, but lately he's started listening to other music—The Wes Montgomery Trio instead of Mercyful Fate and Napalm Death—and he's been reading different books (a lot of the Barry Yourgrau stuff), he's been spotted conversing with strange girls, *other* girls, he's talking to strangers, other people, people other than *our* friends—I fear he may be falling behind a step, or maybe it's me who's falling behind, I fear he may be drifting away

   sometimes I fear I'm changing too much—getting too far from who I should be, and then other times I catch myself fearing that I'm not changing at all, not moving forward, stagnating, getting complacent

   sometimes I think the saddest thing about some people is that you could tell them anything and they would believe you, that they *need* to believe what they're told—like you could shout into the night wind that their mother's an ugly whore, and I swear a lot of people would believe you, and why? well because somebody said it, so it must be true (and I fear that I'm coming to realize that it's the world itself that seems to be an ugly whore—the human condition in general—the prisons around us, our minds, our bodies—but then again I could never really absorb the full picture of the events that float on around me)

   then sometimes I wonder if I'm just thinking too much—too many thoughts cluttering the way, gumming up the works, bogging me down—and sometimes I wonder if I'm one of those poor saps who just feels too much, who just wants too much, needs too much, expects too much, and thus can't focus on just one thing, or maybe I've just lost too much now and don't want anything to ever change in my life ever again, so much that I'm also concerned that I may be missing out on some things, letting things pass by unnoticed—people and events and stuff—as I'm too far gone inside my own mind—too far lost in thought to notice, which is not something to be bragging about or proud of ... and suddenly, in realizing this, the pain builds and slowly squeezes out of me in the form of me (for some reason) shouting into the vast yawning chasm of night the words: "clown penis!!!" as a tortured, anguished wail of frustration, pain, and exasperation, just like always—so if you ever find yourself out in the darkness, on one of your travels, and you hear a faint "clown penis" yelped into the night, shouted out of the vague distance for no real reason and directed at no one in particular, just appearing in the deep blank night as if from out of nowhere, well, it'll probably be from me or one of my future followers, disciples of the lonely darkness, explorers of the emptiness, the wasteland—expeditionaries on another journey into the unknowable

and then it all slips away again

sometimes it feels like the invisible hands of fate are holding us back, keeping us down—other times it feels like the hands of fate are keeping us safe in this insulated back alley world (which we've been pressed and processed into by indifference)—then other times it's as if we're not good enough to walk amongst the sidewalk crowd, in the light—or maybe this private refuge of ours is actually the real world, this dark inside-out nowhere area around us here, the "real" world as it is meant to be—stripped bare of ornamentation and phony artifice, stripped of all pretense, as if there was no-where else to go, no-where left to hide

I look over at dave, standing there off to the side, together with us and yet at the same time alone by himself, kicking dirt in frustration and shame—another night stuck here in the back alley world, another night stuck here with us, another night struggling to get out, another night sent home alone, banished to the darkness, the blankness, the nothingness—back into the wasteland again my friend, back to the places no one else wants—who could blame dave for wanting to break free of his limitations, who could blame him for wanting to grow and evolve, who could blame him for wanting more, for looking to add to his life—and at this moment it feels like I'm the one who's been the hand of fate, as if I'm the one who's keeping him down, forcing my perceptions and insecurities down on him—sure I don't want to lose him to another, losing all that he is and all that he has—his tapes, his old magazines, his staring shimmy, his twitching dance, his *september gurls* tape from big star, his *another girl, another planet* tape from the only ones—but I also don't want to see my friend so down, so lost and alone—as through him I have finally isolated my failures—that I am stagnating here, living in the past, and even if I can't see out of this life, then maybe I can help dave out of his, even if I have to push him out of it—and dave claims to need the practice so that someday he will have his rap refined to a pure degree, the syrup down cold, the remedy at his reach—and I want to give him that chance, because sometimes that's all we get in life, just one chance—I know if I can help him it will put him in the best possible position if and when he gets his one chance with that special and unique someone, he's my friend after all, and I want him to have that, that much anyway, however much that ends up being

and then, as I'm just standing there thinking in all that emptiness of darkness, in the best possible place to be, I watch as dave steps off the sandy trail of alley, out into that vast oily morass of night, entangled, sinking, going down, going under, going into that thick darkness, out to explore that thick who-knows-what wilderness of future, to disappear into that mirror of unknowable, to spiral down into that void—now into the darkness, a pioneer of life, oh courageous heroes

and then he became like a great wind, and strangely enough I never saw him again after that night at the bowling alley—maybe he ran into one of those girls and got entangled in her life, some say he moved away and changed his name, trying to shed the past to start over fresh, I don't rightly know, but now, days and months and seconds and moments later I feel him changing, I feel him becoming like an elusive feeling, that spoiled friendship of loading dock beers and back door alley leanings and winds of night whistling softly through us as we all fade on—he has become like a great crystal vase that has held so many secrets for too long, so many dreams, I simply had to protect them, dave shattering into a million transparent events, a million feelings, a million hopes and dreams and aspirations and lives, all overlapping one another in colorful translucent layers of feelings, refracting tons of new colors, colors no one else ever thought of, I simply had to protect them all, so as not to spill any of them, lose any of them—so as not to spill any secrets ... but then again what do I know, I only know what I see and feel, and how can you trust any of those senses? how can you trust what constantly changes?

for dave granger is in grave danger, for he has just seen a girl (haw ... aahhh ... choke ... gasp ... [whispered hush] a girl mind you ... a girl ...), a young lass who has caught his weary eye, and he's not even met her really—they've never even been formally introduced, not even on the most casual level—he's never even overheard her name in passing conversation—will he ever get to know that elusive and elastic name? so slippery and clean, that epic, operatic, catastrophic name, that tidy and efficient collection of letters—will the cold, exhale of fates that swirl in the shadows ever allow this? will he ever see her again? will their eyes ever meet? will he be able to open his mouth even (imagine that! what courage!) and let escape several rare and precious words? will those magic words ever collect themselves and find their way to daylight and into that warm embrace of her ear? will her feelings at last belong to another? will she forever bruise his fragile and inexperienced heart? will he ever be able to gather the resolve to ever feel this way again? to ever let slip some precious and courageous words? will he ever be able to take that mighty leap of faith and ever risk letting more enormous and elaborately crystalline collections of letters escape the prison of his breath? will he ever be able to handle those enormously cumbersome words ever again? words as difficult to lift as "hello"? (oh, the heft ... oh, the struggle) will he ever dare whisper "hello" again? ... will she ever look deep into his eyes? ... will she ever whisper his name?

that night I have the dream again, the dream of getting sucked back down a dark alley, inhaled, me running down a narrow alley with tall weeds and old tires and garbage cans and stacked pallets on either side, me running through the night, my shadow rippling behind like the black swamp dog of time chasing me down, the alley narrowing, and I'm running and running, the wind rushing with me, my shadow giving chase, hunting me down to swallow me, obliterate me, my running creating more and more wind, my running a whirl-wind, rushing faster and faster, but I don't really know where I'm running to, I'm just rushing along in the darkness, just running and running, rushing in the wind, creating my own wind, until I become the wind, the alley around me blurring in a tunneled stream of speed, and I'm running and running, feeling the cool wind rushing through me, rushing to out-run time, out-run my mistakes, rushing to dave, to plead, please dave, please, don't give your heart away so easily

in the sun

I sigh at ease, looking out at it all. I'm alone in the back of the bus, its loud rattle moving me along. Shadows of leaves dance on the window and on my face as the sun splashes my stare. I shift around as the bus shakes. I bring my hands from my lap to my sides to the top of my legs to under my legs to my pockets and then back to my lap again. And the afternoon sways and rattles and I taste last week in its stale air.

The sun leaks through the holes between leaves as if grainy light dripping in from better places, better times. The deep summer shadows flash on and off while the sun winks through the trees. The sun sits in my lap and takes turns with the shade.

Objects flash by the window—a garbage can, an old engine block, a baseball mitt in the gutter—things people once shared. I notice small birds cleaning themselves in a dark puddle in the gutter. They dip their heads in and come up and shake it all off. Then a stripped bike frame appears, still chained to the leaning stanchion of a street sign—the street sign is missing. And then more objects we need—a wagon missing a wheel, a hubcap, a wheelchair tipped over in the weeds—more things we need to get us around, just strewn about, stripped. A duck standing in an empty parking lot of a boarded-up fast food restaurant. A burnt-out gas station. A three-legged dog. A man missing an arm. He was digging in a garbage can, looking for something. An abandoned house. All of its windows were missing. Someone took them. A chain-link fence without a gate. Just a gap where a gate could be. Things missing, healing. Things lost, strewn about. People missing pieces, disconnected, just strewn about. The bus rattling. The old air.

Things speed by in a blur, people flash on and off in the brightness and dark, illuminated, obscured, the backs of people, people's sides, people turned around, parts of people here and there, some entering shadows, others sticking out, things appearing then disappearing, lost forever, things that are there for a moment and then not there, things that evaporate, things that are held in place, prisoners, things that are loose, rattling around, things that are adrift, free to change, to grow, and things wandering around, lost.

I watch the lawns, bright sun and dark shadows. Lawns to play in, lawns to mow, lawns to dream about and lay in. As I watch, I think of how good that sun can be to you, to warm you, and I think of how cruel that sun can be to you, can expose things, can expose you. I ride with it for a while, then take the photo of us out of my wallet. I hold that photo, work it in my hands, then I set it on my lap. I gaze out the window at all the perfect green lawns and then look down at the photo and then out the window at everything going by again. Blotches of light and dark continue to blink on and off, houses flash by, entire lives, things people share. Then I put that photo back. It's the first time I've had it out in weeks.

I keep this photo of me and Lori in my wallet. It's the only photo I have with me—my favorite, a perfect picture of us when we were together, taken a few days before we moved into the attic of that old green house.

We cleaned that damn upstairs for two days it was so bad. Sleeping on her big mattress, lying together watching TV half the night, working on the garden on summer weekends, stamping on cockroaches together—that summer went by so fast, that upstairs filled up so fast—first the fifteen dollar couch from the Salvation Army, then the shelves from the Goodwill and the air conditioner from some garage sale. I can still smell that upstairs, the curtains Lori made swaying gently, hearing the wind sigh with her long summer dresses flowering around her legs. The clean grass and fresh dirt, that day we called in sick in August and it rained. I remember that rain, it made everything smell so clean and full.

I'm on my way to see her at her friend's house on the other side of town. She's been staying there for a while. Time somehow stands still on the bus. I'm trying to stay calm, and the bus moves so slowly, and I just want everything to go smoothly. I just want to be there with her. I just want everything to be OK, to be like it was.

I sit on my hands in the back, the window open, smelling that rushing breeze, and I picture her running up to me and welcoming me on the sidewalk. And that breeze slaps at my face, cooling me in the shade of the bus. The ride seems to last forever, but I really don't mind. I picture her there. I watch her welcome me at the porch. I feel her arms stretch out, she hugs me tightly. I think she misses me.

I see us go inside. I taste the smell of her neck and her hair and her lemonade as she plays her neighbor's old piano. She can make that weak old thing sing. I could watch her forever, with her head up and eyes closed, the sun glowing behind us in jealousy in that photograph.

That piano was the biggest pain to get up those stupid stairs. I thought we were all gonna die for sure that night Kevin and Josh had to stay over, that thing sunk in the steps. We had to lower Kevin down with a bed sheet to go get beer. He got footprints all over the side of the house on his way back up. Yeah, I thought we'd all die for sure, by a fire or something, with that old piano tilted in those stairs, the one end poking through into the closet below.

I remember the day the photo was taken. The first time I heard her play that old thing. The first time I ever heard her play. The piano had been tucked away in her neighbor's garage. A dusty tarp covered it and she slid it off, telling me about how her and Melinda would hammer away on it when they were kids, before Melinda's accident. It was the first time she'd seen it in years. It looked pretty sad with its green paint peeling and cracked keys. She said she could repaint the flowers and begged we bring it along. I just laid down in the dust of the garage and laughed. And then she started to play. And the sun heard it and came peeking around, lighting the dark corners in a golden haze. And it was like another time, as though we were moving back through the years. Shadows grew and spread and splashed like a bright ocean of paint. And she closed her eyes and that thing came alive to cling to me, to stay with me forever, that damn thing. And I have proof of that in this photo of us as golden explorers in the sun.

It's only about two blocks to her friend's house. The bus hums away and the leaves sway with the breeze in the trees. The trees are so tall and thick and it's so cool under that canopy, in that soft, dreamy tunnel. And I breathe in the leaves and the fresh grass as I move, the sun tickling me through the shade, the wind gently rubbing my face, the sky so amazingly big, stretching out to fill the days ahead.

I walk up the sidewalk, and she steps out onto the porch as I had pictured. She stands holding the wood railing in the sun with a long skirt gently weaving around her legs as always.

Things looked too good I guess. She invites me in. She makes lemonade. But I don't see the piano anywhere, and she doesn't sit by me on the couch as I had thought. She sits on some old chair, so I stretch out on her friend's rug. I hoped we could talk about old times, about last summer, about that house and that piano and all. But every time I try to take us back she pays no attention or starts up about her new classes. Things just looked a little too good I guess. And I can feel the sun outside, warming the old house, shining on the lawns and trees, as if waiting for us, as if wanting to play with us again.

I don't stay long, or it doesn't seem that long anyway. I stand on the porch for a moment after I leave. I look out and the sky feels so long and empty, blushing a dusty rose so far away. I reach into my wallet, slide that photo out and take one long look at it, looking at it for one more time, gazing right through time and falling into it. I remember those days so clearly. Somehow that golden picture of us in the sun seemed so perfect.

I set that photo down carefully, gently leaving it on the wood railing of the porch. Then I step off into the grass.

big baby

It's been a long long week and you're tired. You lay down on the couch for a moment of peace, but just then you get an urgent call from a friend down the block. Your friend is out of breath, "Oh, thank all that is holy, you're home," she sighs, "Our neighbor needs assistance right away... Hurry," and the line goes silent, leaving only an impatient dial tone. You hang up and jog down the block to see what the trouble is. You find your friend in the street next to a running car with its door open.

A well dressed woman runs out of her house to your friend.

"Here," your friend gestures to you, looking at the woman running from the house, as if to indicate: "This one can help," then hops in the car.

"Oh, thank all that is holy," the woman sighs, throwing up her arms, "This way." She spins on her heels and starts back to the house.

You look over to your friend in the car, then back to the house. You shrug and start after the woman, following her around the house to the backyard.

"We need a sitter," the woman huffs, jogging, looking back at you, obviously in a hurry and very concerned about something, "For a while... Not long... Couple hours... Hopefully... Well, you know how it goes..."

You shrug a mild shrug of understanding as you jog around the house, happy to help out a neighbor, happy to be of some use to the day, happy to bank some good Karma. You enter the backyard to find sitting in the middle is a giant baby. He must be twenty feet tall, just sitting there looking down at you with a long, glistening strand of drool hanging from his chin. The baby is a chubby one, wearing only what looks like a large bed sheet for a diaper.

"That's Chester," the woman slows, gesturing up to the great baby, "He can be quite a handful at times."

You slow to a stop. Your jaw drops into a frozen, mouth-open stare. You can't take your eyes off him. You don't realize it right off, but your hands are on the sides of your face, slowly compressing your cheeks. You squeal a slight whine of anguish, "Eeeeemmmmm," as if something mechanical deep inside you has suddenly rattled loose. Your knees weaken to buckle and you sink ever so slightly, slowly imploding.

"Thanks," the woman loops around without even stopping and dashes back around the house, "We'll be back later," she calls, not defining when "later" might be.

You hear a distant car door slam and a car scream away as if fleeing a bank robbery.

The baby looks down on you, drooling a long stream of drool, and reaches for you. You just freeze. The sight is awe inspiring. The majesty of it all—a baby, life itself, the weight, the heft, the fresh innocence of crystal clear drool. The baby picks you up and brings you in close. His stubby hand is warm and so slimy with drool you almost slide right through as he brings you in and holds you tightly, warmly. He leans in to look you over. Then he lowers his arm to rest you on his knee. And there you sit, in the clammy grip of a giant baby in a backyard.

Without moving, the baby continues to look you over, considering you for some unknowable baby reason. He pulls you in close again, gives you another big look-see. Then looks around suspiciously, from side to side to see if anyone else is around. He leans back in and whispers, "Tell me your secrets."

For some reason a grand wave of relief and fulfillment sweeps over you, emptying from you as if a great weight of fluid has been released from within, as if you've been waiting your entire life for someone to say that to you, to relieve you of your invisible burdens, burdens building up and loading you down that you never even realized were there. Or maybe you're just happy to be of service, to finally be able to help someone who really deserves it. You sigh a fulfilled sigh, taking in the calm that is sweeping over you.

And then you notice, in the large field of blank white skin next to you, a little person deep inside, reflected in the drool at his sides as if you were looking into a storefront window, all glistening and slick. The little person inside floats nearer to you, growing a little bigger, floating closer to the surface. "Lies... I need lies," it says, looking at you, then receding back into the distance, and then into nothing.

You relax and breathe at ease, as if you've been constrained your whole life, as if something has always been gripping you tightly, and now is finally able to let you go, only you hadn't realized until just now. You exhale, "Oh, thank you, Big Baby," you nod up to the baby in polite appreciation, an expression of great relief releases your face, as if held captive there for years. You burst out, "I never had a cool name, you know, like 'Luke' or 'Chet'. A cool name draws in other cool things. A cool name opens doors... I like to dress up as a banana and go to church. Any church... I like to dress up as an old grandma lady of yesteryear and start fires... I like to phone people at random and tell lies, lies and lies and lies, and then even more lies. Torrents of lies. Lies that I hope will come true... I like to convince people not to hang out with other people, trying to convince them that everyone else is bad, that I'm the good one, the only good one, the one they should pick... Usually I start by flattering them, and listening to them, that creates an opening... I like to steal cars and drive them into the river... I like to watch as they slowly go under, much like watching my life go under, a great weight pushing all the bad things away, pushing things down, under a murky, dark sludge of polluted water, as if to hide things, bury things... I made a couch out of tampons. I was tired of having to go out late at night for my lady, so I just bought a ton one time, cleaned out a mess of stores, formed them into a couch. Now if she asks me to go out late at night to get some for her, and I mean always late at night, real real late, I just peel one from the couch and reach it over to her, 'Here, knock yourself out,' I nod... I go to the all-night hardware store in the wee hours and sit in my car and watch the insomniacs as they contemplate their various choices of tile. Always so many choices. Headache inducing choices. Face contorting choices. And yet never enough choices... And I sit in my car and weep. Weep for all the lost choices..." You stop for a moment to wonder if the baby, or the person deep inside, realizes if these are truths or lies that you're spilling out. Will they be able to pull the truths from the lies and the lies from the truths? Will they be able to untangle it all? You draw up a deep breath, "I drive a fancy car just to impress people. So people will be jealous of me... I don't give money to charity, I dump it all into my over-compensation-mobile. So as to finally prove that I'm better than everyone else. So people will assume I'm successful, better than all the others, and thus want to be around me, making me feel good. And since I'm better than all the others, I must be smarter than them. Clearly that is obvious. So what I say and think is therefore more important and more truthful than all the others... My insights, my opinions, become fact, become real..."

The big baby nods politely, thoughtfully, and smiles at all this, as if secrets are some type of knowledge, experience, or nourishment he'll need later in life. Maybe he'll be able to shape them into something and give that to someone in the future. Maybe this knowledge will make him smarter, more prepared, able to avoid future calamities and maladies. It's odd the things we see as sustenance.

Another man sheepishly creeps into the backyard. "Big Baby... Big Baby..." he whispers cautiously, bent over and ducking, as if afraid, as if ashamed, as if expecting to be hit with the wrong end of the crap stick of life at any moment, as if he'd been bullied and ridiculed by insecure hate mongers and halfwits his entire life, as if he needs a hug, a pat on the back, a kind word spoken warmly in his direction, as if the great sad drunken clown of life has peed on his back door his entire life. "...Will... Will you... Will you hold me? ... Release my inner secrets and expectations that bog me down, that get in the way... Release my lies?"

The baby looks over, leans down, reaches...

The man slowly slinks to the baby, still looking around.

The baby plucks the sheepish man from the shadows, raises him into the light, pulls him in close, sets him on his other knee, leans in. "Tell me your secrets," the big baby whispers.

Then another man sneaks into the backyard from the alley, looking around to make sure he has not been followed. This one also looks ashamed, burdened, as he slowly creeps around the garage. "Big Baby... Big Baby..." he whispers, "It's been a long long week..."

You notice the baby's skin is a pure field without a mark on it. You see your reflection in it, and the reflection of the other man, reflections in the glistening drool on his sides. But the reflected faces are yammering on, sort of mumbling. "What are they saying?" you nod over to the other man.

"Lies," he nods back, "It needs lies," he shrugs as if he doesn't know why. "It's wonderful, isn't it? The chatter. The fog of lies."

The big baby slowly begins to rise. His stubby arms set both of you down. At first you think he is standing to toddle off, but he keeps going up. Up and up he rises, suddenly lifting off the grass as if to float.

"Lies," the second man whispers in a desperate squeal, "More lies... He needs more... Quickly..." He rushes forward, jumping to grab onto one of the big baby's toes. He hangs there for a moment, then begins to wiggle and tug downward. The weight of the second man slowly pulls the baby back down.

The other man, the first one, leaps forward and jumps to grab another toe, pulling the baby back into the center of the yard. "Whew, that was a close one."

The baby just smiles and plops back down, each man jumping up to sit on the baby's chubby, slimy thighs. "...And failures," the baby nods and coos, "Tell me your failures."

"I've never been married. I fail constantly. Nothing but failures. A parade of failures," one of the men begins. You can't tell which man is which now as they both look about the same, or close enough anyway. "I work a job that is impossible to be good at. The best you can do is not be bad... And my bosses expect perfection, home runs..."

The other one starts in: "Nothing I do ever works out... Nothing... My life is a train wreck," he squeaks. "...So much so that I've stopped trying all together. Why even bother any more... All I do now is cry."

The baby looks off to the horizon, to the distant treetops and roofs, and nods, listening as they both speak at once, each staring down and shaking their heads in confusion and disappointment, as if examining a potato salad that's gone unexpectedly bad.

They babble at the same time, just talking and talking, almost as if about nothing at all, their voices intertwine, the sounds joining to drone hypnotically, as if to let the baby know that he is alive, that he exists—as if to weigh the baby down with existence.

"I'm a failure. A full-on calamity ... so much so that I'm afraid to even do anything now, afraid to try anything. I mean, why even bother? "

"As am I, though even more so. Because I'm scared... I'm a coward..."

"Who's the bigger baby? Well obviously it's me, that can not be denied..."

"I will never amount to anything... It's all gone now, all my opportunities, all my chances, slowly fading, slowly slipping away..."

"I find myself dwelling on the negatives. It's like I'm stuck to tarpaper and can't get away from it. Why is my insurance so high? Why don't I get more vacation days? ..."

"It's hard for me to dwell on the good things too. Why can't I see the positives more, the possibilities? ... Maybe that's the key to it all, what holds it all together..."

"Did I make the right choices? ..."

You realize you are not meant for such situations, some things are just too big to grasp. You're just not built to tune in to what their particular problems or needs are at this time, so you slowly step back, into the shadow of the garage, to give them some space. You sit in the grass and lean against the garage, waiting the return of the parents.

Slowly you gaze off to the hazy distance, looking to the sky, because the clouds are your favorite things ever, always reliable, always interesting, always changing. The sky is a thin baby blue, with wisps of fuzzy white. There are only a few stray clouds about, as if kingdoms you could explore if only you could reach them. Just three puddles of clouds, randomly scattered. But then you notice, way up in the sky, some small shapes. You squint to see, and they come into focus as baby shapes—more giant babies, glistening and bright, floating by on the breeze, way up there. You locate three—no, wait, four, then five ... then six ... and then another, and maybe another way off—at least seven giant babies gliding on the breeze, wobbling like large balloons, off to who knows where.

moonlight (althea)

It's very late. I'm walking home. The moon hangs on the horizon, illuminating everything in a ghostly, silvery haze. The washed-out landscape becomes wintry in this grainy light. Up ahead I notice some maidens gently twirling in the middle of the crossing of two cobblestone roads. Their lacy gowns glow in the light of the bright moon. I can't believe my eyes, for I have stumbled upon a host of beautiful, heavenly maidens spinning in the moonlight, their gowns shining like lanterns.

I dash to the ditch at the side of the road. I hide behind the thick grey trunk of a tree. I watch in awe as they twirl and leap in the air, slowly making their way up the walk to a stone house. They dance on the lawn in front of this little house, backs bending, arms swaying, hair swishing. Their arms and backs undulate like liquid. They snake in through an open window and moments later emerge again, this time passing a sleeping man through the window. The curtains blow in the night's breath as they support the man with their hands. The man appears to be sleeping, as if they've lulled him far away. They support him above their heads, gently carrying him out into the front yard. The bright moonlight illuminates them with a silvery shine.

The women dance, presenting him to the night, turning and spinning through the yard, floating the man into the field at the edge of town. Little pixies appear at their feet, somersaulting and tumbling. Delicate little butterflies flutter out from under the maidens' gowns to be illuminated by the night's sun as they all disappear into the tall grass of the clearing.

I follow them, silently creeping low and quick, in and out of the moon's shadows, ducking behind large rocks, trees, and tall grass. But I soon lose them in the height and darkness of the alfalfa field. So I slink back to the ditch to await their return behind the first tree I hid behind when I first saw them. The next morning I wake up, curled in the long, coarse grass under the tree. I must've fallen asleep. The morning is bright and dry. I crawl up the side of the ditch, just in time to catch the man they had carried. He is leaving his house and making his way to work in the morning.

I follow him into the center of our village, through narrow alleys and over a small arching stone bridge. He enters a little store. He is a stocky man, portly, stout. Through the large storefront window, I watch as he takes off his hat and puts on an apron in a butcher shop. I go in and begin looking around, slowly starting up a conversation with an elderly woman at the counter. The stout man is there, tending to his stock. Meat products hang all around in the bright market. There are sharp silver knives of all kinds on pegs up on the yellow tile walls. There are animals lying stacked on a table in back. It looks as though the animals are sleeping. Rabbits and large birds hang in rows from the ceiling.

I begin talking about last night and an unusual dream that I had. I didn't really have a strange dream, I just want to see if the stout man remembers what happened to him in the field the night before, so I would know what had happened when they disappeared into the darkness.

Then I turn to ask the old lady if she has strange, foggy dreams at times. She nods and shrugs quietly as if to say, 'yeah, sometimes, I suppose.' Then I look over to the stout butcher and ask him, and he just shakes his head as he is concentrating on wrapping the older woman's meat.

The butcher answers, "No. No. Not too much. I don't really dream much at all. Now that you mention it, I don't recall ever experiencing the full extent of a dream in my entire life. Only some faint flashes, I guess. I don't even think I'd know what one would be like."

Talk of this nature makes me anxious. I realize that I want all of my dreams, every last one of them. And I want the butcher to have his. He deserves them after all, as if each were an internal organ, as if each were a mini adventure you could revisit from time to time. And now I'm getting nervous that someone might make off with one of my dreams and never return with it. And how would I ever know if someone ever did? Or what if there were other things like dreams that I've never experienced because someone is taking those away from me? What if there were all manner of things out there that I'm missing out on?

"Oh, my, you've never ever had a dream before?" the old lady looks up.

"Emm, no. Not really. Can't say that I have," the butcher shrugs, "Not a single one in all my life. It's more like I wake up some mornings and it feels like I'm missing some-thing—just a little tingle of a feeling, a vague incomplete-ness—like someone has stolen a dream from me, like I have this fresh little empty space inside of me where a dream should've been, as if someone has run off with a dream of mine. But run off to where? And what would someone do with a dream of mine? Where would you keep it?"

"I'd stretch it out to create a sail, and then use it to float off to who knows where," I advise.

"Would it be valuable? Could you sell it for a tidy profit?" the butcher shrugs.

"Could you paste it together with pieces of other dreams to create even greater, more elaborate dreams?" the old lady wonders.

And soon others in the shop join in. "Could you keep it in your wallet to show others at parties and social gatherings?"

"Could you hang it on your wall, as if showing off an expansive, panoramic vista?"

"Could you pass it around for your friends and neighbors to share?"

Gradually the ladies leave, and I can't help thinking they look a little like the fair maidens from the night before, but older versions of them—as if they could change to their younger selves on full mooned nights, as if they could play in the moonlight forever.

shiny things

hooray for all the children

All the other children called him froggy. "He looks like a frog," they'd say. "If you squint real hard," they'd say. "Those drab green clothes. He has that froggy way about him," they'd say. "That pond smell; that bull-legged way about him; those puffy jowls; that mysteriously thin straight line for a mouth; the bulging, ping-pong-ball eyes; the weak chin; the sloping forehead; the manner in which the back of his head is so small; that pinhead quality about him, that football shaped face, that blank expression, that expressionless stare, and those warts, oh those warts, what a spectacular collection..."

His clothes were too old, too green, too small, too tight, too smelly—a weird momma's boy smell. His hair too greasy, too matted. His head was like a lopsided lump of fruit rolling on bony, handlebar shoulders. His freckles were mere blights of disorganized rust tripping across his pale face.

The children would push him down the stairs. And kick his books. They'd have contests. In the halls they'd give him tremendous snuggies, reaching into his outdated, olive pants to yank up his underwear from behind. They'd hoist him to his tippy-toes, tapping a quick dance on the hard terrazzo floor, not relieving him until his face achieved a specific shade of crimson.

At recess he would often wander off the school grounds down to the river where he could find peace in the rocks that he would collect. His favorites were the aggies, with their swirls of colors spinning together as one perfect jewel. He would have to sneak back carefully, hiding the rocks in his unfashionably dark socks as the children would often catch him and make him swallow his treasures.

On field trips they would cram red-hots up his nose. On

the playground they would funnel sand through their cupped hands into his throat. And they would hold contests to see how far they could throw him. It was a game soon dubbed "catapult." On the bus home they'd make him eat sticks and leaves and worms because, they figured, frogs liked sticks and leaves and worms.

They'd make him eat sawdust. They'd pour glue in his hair. They'd fill his locker with dead squirrels after they'd fermented them in the sun. They'd put his head in the toilet and flush the lever, insuring that all the girls, with their little electric smiles, would run away from him. They'd make up songs about him—choruses, operas, vast arias, tender lullabies, cute rhyming jingles, and clever limericks with tiny little hooks. And that was all just on Tuesdays.

He was an easy target, so thin he couldn't fight back—what was the use? It only made things worse. They cemented the social order with their gossip. And as the propaganda swelled, even the teachers began to turn against him, casually referring to him as froggy, whether he was around or not.

Later in life froggy staggered off to college where he ultimately prospered in the concrete industry, perhaps inspired by all the aggregate he passed through his system earlier in life on that vast, bright, hot, lonely, magnifying glass of a playground.

He never married, but had squirrels for pets and that alchemy business—mixing different things together to construct something new and solid—bridges and roads and buildings and big, solid, heavy things—monuments that would last for years, monuments that reached into the future, far beyond anyone's grasp, reaching far beyond anyone's vision. He'd build them so he could be there himself, far far away, in another place none of us could even imagine, in a place none of us could touch.

He was getting pretty large in the region—state contracts, unions, politicians, that sort of thing. I'd see his photo in the paper every now and then, all curt and natty now. He was into pretty much everything. For a long time I felt he was concentrating his efforts into an endeavor that, frankly, was a size or so too large for his personality. I figured he'd end up becoming a biology professor or maybe a Department of Natural Resources guy. I just figured he'd be happier that way—alone in the weeds by some forgotten stream.

That's about the time I seem to have felt it began to happen. One day I was reading the newspaper. I was reading about an old classmate who mysteriously disappeared. Eventually he turned up in over 3000 cans of a popular brand of tuna. A horrible fate to be sure, and amplified by the fact that the guy was notoriously reputed to detest tuna.

Then one day another classmate was found several blocks from town, filled with sand, his mouth and nose caulked shut with insulating sealant. Then there was that guy they discovered tarred over in the road, his arms stretched out, trying to cover his head. And another they happened upon who was glued to a wall. As they peeled him off, they noticed he was unusually heavy. The X-rays proved their speculation—that he had been filled with rocks. They discovered another classmate in a field two counties over. The medical examiner said it was as if he'd been catapulted into the air and had traveled a great distance. Another was found floating down a stream—flat as an oak leaf, but curled up at the ends, as if he'd been steamrollered. Another guy came home from work one day and discovered that his house was completely gone—not a crumb, not a thread, not a piece of lint left of it. The spot where his house was supposed to be was all flat and covered with sod. Squirrels foraged for nuts in the leaves where his house should've been. His house was missing, gone, vanished, and they never found any of it—all his belongings, his entire life erased. One gal walked out to her driveway one morning to find their camper, boat, and three family cars crushed into hay bale sized crinkly metal cubes. Each crumpled, gleaming, jazzy metal chunk was neatly returned to its spot on the driveway and next to the garage. Eventually she had the metal chunks brought downstairs to use as furniture in their pool room. Another guy was unfortunate enough to have found himself just a little too close to a brick making machine. It is believed he was eventually distributed all over the state. Perhaps he is a part of your new patio or garage.

There was a lot of talk around town, suspicious murmurs and rumors and that sort. Was it all just coincidence? A bad run of fate? Bad hoodoo? Why couldn't people leave well enough alone? The past is just best left in the past. Let bygones be bygones. Why hold on to things? Water under the bridge and all that after all.

There was a lot of talk about that overweight kid. What was his name? They say froggy gave him the money to buy the towing company he worked at. Now I don't know if all that was true, but every time I'm out and about—running errands or what have you—and I can't find my car, maybe two or three times a year, it always seems to turn up in the city impound lot.

This was all well and good, I thought, sitting comfortably, observing from the safe distance of my cozy reading chair in my living room in the suburbs. From time to time classmates of ours would pop up in the paper, stuffed in this device or caught in that, found in a grassy field just outside of town, their bodies a distorted mystery to be unraveled. Hooray! I say. Hooray for all the children! Hooray for froggy!

And then the other night I was watching television tucked safely away in my living room. The game was just getting good when I felt a truck rumbling up—a big truck sneaking up the block. I watched, peeking through the drapes in my suburban paranoia as a large, heavy-duty cement truck squeaked to a shuttering stop in front of my driveway. I could feel that heavy beast idling in my chest, oscillating back and forth, to and fro, coiled up with a rapid pulse.

It was pitch black out. The truck's lights weren't on. The damn monster revved to growl and purr menacingly for a few moments, and then slowly lurched forward to creep out of sight in a huff of exhaust.

The next morning word spread from down the block that a distant classmate of mine awoke to find his pool filled with rotting, dead frogs. They had to shovel them out with snow shovels and pitchforks. It took all weekend to load them into plastic garbage bags. Eventually they had to retile the entire pool.

About a week later I returned from a business trip in which I was able to bring my family along. We got in late. The world was dark and quiet. Everything so quiet and still, frozen in a peace I wouldn't even want to describe, a peace I wouldn't want to disturb. I laid in bed with my eyes open, and I felt that peace settling inside of me like the leaves drifting off the trees to blow away with the wind.

The next morning I awoke very early to retrieve my morning paper. The sun was just creeping up over the city, shadows stretching to search for new homes, pushing against the lazy purple and green horizon.

I opened my door to find my front step stretching out before me. It had grown to cover the yard, the entire yard smoothly entombed under a four inch blanket of white concrete, yawning exquisitely out to the street, as smooth and shiny as a baby's backside.

I was stunned, and yet strangely exhilarated.

I stepped out onto it in mouth-open wonder. My slippers shuffled on its drying softness. As I walked, leaves pittered with the breeze across its smooth, hard surface.

The craftsmanship was inspiring—the way it terminated perfectly at the street with a crisp, sharp edge. The way it coated the trees twelve feet up in a snug, warm glove. I turned to discover they had completed much of the siding as well, concrete creeping up with crude plywood forms bolted in and tied back with rusting, blushing, threaded rods—up, up, up and over and back down the other side in some places.

Marvelous!

Tremendous!

Applause! Applause!

Encore!

I was moved.

Later, I discovered they had ambitiously completed the entire backyard as well, hugging the flower beds, blanketing the garden, covering my boat, hiding my wife's car under a soft hush of concrete. It was an impressive sight. Poor Sparky, he sat there stoically, an attentive statue, a mere bump in the middle of the backyard. I stood there in the sparkling morning sun in my soft flannel pajamas—the ones beautifully imprinted with the faces of notorious underworld crime figures. I felt that concrete under me, my skin getting warm as if I were Sparky, preserved in time, wearing it forever as it spread out to discover new lives, new events, new times.

I can't recall if I ever did anything to poor old froggy—perhaps I did, or maybe I did not. But I was there and that was enough for me. Hooray, I say. Hooray for all the children, for we have taught one another well.

I went back inside and gently climbed back into bed as if steadying myself into a small rowboat, careful not to wake even the littlest of things. I closed my eyes as if after an unfavorable dream, as if to clean that ugly mirror of time, as if to wipe it all away, hoping to awaken with everything returned as fresh and bright as it had always been.

Astrological shadows crawled across the ceiling—constellations of the rising sun projecting through the enthusiastic fall leaves. But all I could think of were the shadows on the patio lawn and froggy as a child, revving that truck, driving it in his mind.

riding the range with the cowboy spies

His dad's light green '73 Chevy pickup bounced us through the darkness.

"Literature?"

"Yeah, you know—books and stuff... Art. The meaning of life. Shit like that."

"Why?"

"...I think I'd like ta try an' figure out this life."

"Oh, yeah. Good luck with that."

"Thought I'd give it a start. While I'm young..." I stretched open a bag of peanuts in my lap. "I figure with everything that's been written down, there's got to be some truth, some answers in all that... They say literature expresses sentiments commonly held by individual cultures," I shrugged. Tiny lights in the distance passed the window. "It'd be nice to understand things."

"So do nudie mags..." Jess tugged a swallow of beer "...and television commercials."

"So maybe I'll end up working in advertising. Who knows... They say popular culture can provide a means for participating in the general sorrow of all." I popped some peanuts into my mouth and looked out the side window. Drops of rain speckled the windows. It was immensely dark, unimaginably dark and nothing was out there. It was all just blank. Everything that passed looked the same—empty fields and gray blob after gray blob, leaving only distant, murky shadows of things. "There's some decent jobs in propaganda and brainwashing these days. They're 'artist's of the people' too ya know."

"Yeah..." Jess looked up, into the darkness as more sprinkles appeared on the windshield. "Those teachers 'll brainwash ya one way or another... For sure... That's all yer payin' 'em for. Why'd ya wanna give somebody money to tell ya what ta think?"

"Aw, It's not like that... Not like high school—there's a lot more interaction and choices. Those so called 'weirdo artists' I've been looking into at that state run asylum, as you refer to it, have been trying to retrieve life from a spiritual wasteland that many cultures evolve into, alienating its..."

"I'm not alienated," he said to himself.

"I never said you were," I popped more peanuts into my mouth.

"Well, I'm not..."

"So don't be... I didn't say..."

"I'm very much grounded and connected and..."

"I'm just explaining their..."

"Schools. All they do is bang out clones. Mindless drones who can't think for themselves." He sped up, through an intersection. The pickup bounced us through a flashing red light that was strung above the center of a crossroad. Under the light the street glistened a dark red. The beginning of Judas Priest's "Heading Out to the Highway" throbbed around the cab from the tape deck, and for a moment that red light spun in the cab with the beginning riff.

"Uh." I exhaled as the truck bounced us. "Can ya drive a little faster?"

"Hey, some day... " he patted the top of the steering wheel as the truck rattled, "...all this will all be mine."

"Great... Anyway, those artists don't feel it's fashionable to be unpopular. It's just some of 'em feel their most profound expressions are seen as incoherent blithering, the struggle to rescue human meaning from loss, pull truth from artifice. That's why you think they're weird."

"No, I think they're weird because they talk goofy. Dress funny. Probably even smell funny... Being different isn't any big trick, you know... Mess up your hair, wear bright red pants. Really tight pants. It reeks of effort. Why try that hard? It's nothing that special."

"Maybe they're just looking for different ways of seeing the world, other means of expressing and understanding this huge place. Trying to put it all together, examine life, make sense of things."

"They're weird. Therefore they're weirdoes."

"Sounds like you're jealous."

"Hey, it doesn't take a genius not to wash or comb your hair."

"There's more to them than their shoes and haircuts... They're about contemplation and ideas. Discovery. Expanding knowledge. Looking really deep. It's not so much about values necessarily. What you value. What your lifestyle is."

"Maybe they smell funny."

"Well, that's one way to cut yourself off from common humanity."

"I like common things..." he sighed.

"I know. And I don't see 'suffering' as a common experience of life. I mean, I don't believe that suffering 'ennobles,' or anything. That existence is suffering, that suffering is caused by desire. Sometimes there's just... I don't know... pain, uncertainty. Sometimes it's hard to know what to want."

"Pain ain't always so bad. It's there so you know you're alive. And it always goes away. Any setback is only temporary anyway. So why dwell on it." He cranked up the volume on Judas Priest's "Don't Go" as a yellow streetlight flashed above. The golden light skimmed the puddles in the road and circled inside the truck with an amber glow. And everything else was quiet and dark.

"Everything seems so damn important to you. Not everything has to mean something, you know," Jess swigged his beer. "See here, there's another difference—right here," he pointed his beer to the tiny lights on the dash. "...All that weak fag music you've been poisoned by, lo these last few months. 'Don't go,' now there's a song... It's more than a song, it's a truth. An' that's all I ever needed... No questions, no answers, just the straight truth, no fancy jive, no hidden b.s... Not everything has to have some deep meaning to it, you know. There's no deep meaning to absolutely everything, peanut butter, popcorn, the wind in the air."

"No, but it's good to exercise your brain, see things in new ways, develop good critical thinking skills," I searched the blank landscape. "And music is about all I have. 'Shake Some Action' by the Flaming Groovies. Now there's a song."

"What's in the wind? Huh? Life's too weird to try an' uncover hidden things anyway, man. You're either free, or tied down. An' those that think they got 're always lookin' down on those that don't. Pretenders, posers, liars, sellers of their own b.s. ppffff... You know what freedom is? Not having responsibilities. Not having to live by a clock, by someone's arbitrary rules and expectations... Me, hey. I'm a free man."

"So you're a free man?"

"Yeah."

"Free ta do what?"

"Last night I climbed a tree naked. No lie, pal. Three in the morning and drunk as a sailor on payday... I fell asleep up there an' some little kid woke me by throwin' rocks at me. I woke up and there I was, clingin' to a branch. Found my clothes down the alley, folded neat, stacked tight... Two days ago I woke up in a closet of someone I didn't even know. I can't even remember how I got there... Last week I woke up in somebody's garden. Some kid woke me by pokin' me with a broom handle. Claimed I was lightin' off bottle rockets in his yard in the middle of the night and that I let him watch from his bedroom window... I don't even remember having any bottle rockets or where I took them from... This morning I had skittles and potato chips for breakfast... Tonight feels like another 'wake up in the neighbor's garden' kind of nights... Now *that's* freedom."

I sang quietly to myself, "*shake. Some action's what I need. So let me bust out at full speed. 'Cause I'm sure that's all I need. To make it aaalllllllright...* I wonder, is that a sad song, or a happy song? ... Probably depends on what mood you're in."

"Who you tryin' to impress?" Jess sighed.

"What?"

"Why you so dressed up?" Jess popped a bubble with his gum.

"I'm not," I shrugged, looking out at it all—the endless darkness at my side.

"You're wearin' a new shirt."

"So?"

"So... Where're your old clothes?"

"This is old."

Jess shook his head and sighed to himself, "Too bright."

"I like the colors," I sighed to myself. "...Maybe I'll end up teaching."

"Who are you to be telling anyone else what to think?"

"I'm me," I shrugged, "...I'm just saying... You gotta do something."

"Where you gonna teach? ...Joe's Butt College? ..." Jess leaned closer to the steering wheel, resting his arm on top of it, then placing his chin on top of his arm. "That new wave shit makes a guy go soft ... down there, ya know. Seriously. I wouldn't mess with that shit, man. You don't know what you're messin' with there... It's weak, gutless."

I looked over the darkness. "Chicks dig that shit."

Jess snapped his gum. "Yeah?"

"They seem to," I shrugged.

"Hmmm," he leaned back, reached down, and cracked open another beer.

"An all those artists too... Plays. Films. Shit like that... But that doesn't necessarily make them pretentious snobs 'r anything." I returned my attention to the dark window beside me. "Well, some of 'em."

There were little things out there, everything so dark and gray—the ground and sky, all blending together. It all seemed so far away, so distant. I watched my face reflected in the window, reflected in the sky, reflected back at me in that distance, in the dark clouds and in the dark, empty fields, in the future and in the past, vague and uncertain.

"Man, out here I'm a fuckin' freak... All those narrow minded rednecks."

"How's the city?"

"I'm just another self-indulgent dorm room philosopher. No big deal. That's the thing with the city, you're a face in the crowd, and nobody cares," I shake my head. "Everyone's out for themselves."

Another wave of rain sprinkled the windshield again.

"So you're just tryin' ta figure it all out, huh?"

"Just girls first, then I'll take on the rest of life."

"Yeah, good luck with the both a them... That'll keep ya busy for a while..." Jess swung the bottle up to his mouth and back down between his legs. "There's just life man, no figurin' it out, no negotiating with it, no changing it, it's just there... let it be."

Then I realized I had been silent for a long while. I had been thinking. The road buzzed under us as we sped through the night. Finally I wondered out loud: "What do you suppose this place is all about?"

"Life? The planet earth?"

"No. No. This place. Here."

Jess was quiet for a while, thinking about it, then he finally said: "Out here. It's about space. Pure, clean space. The beauty in its vast stretches of emptiness. That uncluttered contemplation. You can fill it with whatever you'd like, whatever that happens to be at the moment... Space. Look at all of it. It's all so calm, serene... so beautiful... But the best thing about it is its promise, that it'll always be there, waiting, ready to be filled... It's got that optimism about it, that potential."

"You're quite the modernist, Jess."

"What's that suppose' ta mean? ...I'm a treasure."

"Nothing. It doesn't mean anything... I was just thinking about how this place could mean different things to different people. How everyone sees things differently. How there's a lot of ways to see something, sometimes all at the same time."

"The city's just too damn crowded. All that sprawl and ugly, wasted space. It all looks the same. It's all the same thing over and over and over."

"Yeah, I know what ya mean. But that's the suburbs... The city... The city's bubbling with new ideas. And more new ones forming under those. All the ideas are new there. Everything's shiny and new."

The bar was remarkably crowded, even though it was pretty early. I was so busy with school I forgot it was Friday. I also forgot some of the mills were back up and running. That must've been why it was so full.

"So how's your dad been?" I shouted as we shuffled through, between flannel and leather and denim, our beers from the truck swinging at our sides. I looked around. The ratio was bad—the ratio between girls and guys. It felt like there was one girl for every ten guys. Just like always.

Jess nodded over to a less crowded area over by the back door. I could barely make out the pool tables and jukebox in the small back room for all the bodies crammed in. I couldn't even see the paneled walls or cheesy beer posters.

"Yeah, ah, you know—about the same. His temper's still so bad we've had to get cheap furniture from the Salvation Army for him to smash. The garage is his best smashin' place..."

"Yeah?"

"It's no big secret. I swear he'd bust that shit up all day if he could. Sometimes I find 'im just layin' out there, asleep, entangled in splinters. Torn fabric. Stuffing everywhere. No lie, hey," he leaned against the wall next to the back door. "An' my mom, she's just as bad. Every now and then I'll walk into a room and there she'll be, on the floor crying. I mean, I don't even know what to do. I take a step to her, but she always just turns her head away and waves me off. It's very confusing. I tell ya, I gotta get outta there, man... I swear my mom learned German just so they could fight without worrying me."

I leaned against the wall next to him and shook my head.

"So, when's the funeral tomorrow?" I scratched my chin, then rubbed my cheek.

"I think at one. I hope it's early," Jess swung his beer from his side up to his mouth and back down again. "Get it over with."

"Yeah," I looked around.

"I just can't believe it. He goes off to the army and gets kacked in a truck accident," we looked into the crowd. "How does that happen?"

"Just does. How's his folks doin'?"

"Ppffff, how do ya think. They all but sent him over there. You know how he was ... he couldn't wait to get over there. The guy had no opinions of his own, just ... just whatever was out there. He'd buy into anything."

"I still can't believe it," I shook my head.

We leaned there for a while and watched everyone, looking for people we knew. It was nice to be in a warm place. I hadn't been back in a couple of months and now it all looked sort of different somehow. It was nice to be back, sort of familiar and comforting, but sort of faded and different. It was starting to look old to me now. Not fresh or bright, like it used to at one time.

Finally, some girl I'd never seen before stopped in front of Jess. They started talking but I had them tuned out, just looking into the crowd.

"...you see, right there, right there, there's another reason you should dump that guy," Jess pointed his beer at her for effect. "That's just one more reason right there," he said as she slid away. She looked back and waved and he nodded back to her and she disappeared into the crowd.

"She didn't even notice I was here."

"Yeah, yer doin' a great job a blendin' in."

"You want every girl to be in love with you, but not every girl is gonna be in love with you..."

"No? That's too bad."

"You can't love every single girl. Only one at a time."

"OK, one at a time. One tonight and then another one later on tonight."

"You don't have to be so competitive. You're just wasting time that could be invested in ... in something real."

"Lookit her. Who's that?" he whispered as he nudged me.

"...that could really get you somewhere, that could really bring you something..."

"They drive me crazy. I swear they drive me crazy. Every last one of 'em. Just look at 'em," he drank. "Them and all their rules."

"Maybe they just have expectations."

"Expectations 'll get your ass into some disappointments man, always expectin' shit."

"Whatever... Anyway, just stay away from that Jen girl, she's mine."

"No, I'm still gonna talk ta her. She likes me."

"She's just being nice. Polite."

"She's bein' nice because she likes me," he pointed to some girl I'd never seen before. "Now that... Now that's life."

"Man, they keep gettin' younger an' younger."

"Yeah, ain't it great."

A group of people who were a couple of grades younger than us looked over to us. I know they were talking about Danny. And I didn't want to say anything, but I hoped a lot of people were going to show up tomorrow. I hoped it for him... But for myself, well, I hoped it would just be me and Jess. And that it would go by fast.

"Let's get outta here," I finally said, as if to get away from all of them, as if to get away from tomorrow.

"You like this place," Jess gestured, as if this were a present to me. "That's why I brought you. You said this was perfect. The perfect place."

I shook my head. "Everything's different now," I shrugged. "It doesn't feel right." That was the thing with Jess—I'd known him so long that talking to him was like talking to myself. Talking to him was like thinking out loud, like being free—like being free of myself.

"Ah, yer just tired that's all. Give it a minute... I think we're supposed to be here."

"Yeah, I know, I think he'd want us to hang out here. Remember the good times, figure it out."

"There's nuthin' ta figure out. It is what it is—nothing more, nothing less."

The waitress came around. Jess shrugged at me and we ordered a second round.

"What about her?" he asked as the waitress disappeared back into the crowd.

"Too old."

"How's that asylum been treatin' ya?" he snapped his gum.

"Busy. Time's just flyin' by."

"You said you liked school, liked keepin' busy."

"I did ... but now I don't know, I ... I don't know ... I just feel outta whack... This is boring, let's get outta here."

"These guys're almost done," Jess lazily swung his beer to a pool table. "Lookit that guy," he laughed. "Just lookit 'im. No way man, No way... Ohhhhh. OK, well, maybe," he shifted his back, still leaning against the wall.

"Let's get outta here," I examined the crowd, looking for someone familiar I guess, but they all looked the same, just one mass.

Jess swallowed a big gulp of beer, a big deep swig. "We've been here a million times," he exhaled.

"It doesn't feel the same," I shook my head. "Not like I thought it would..."

"It's the same," he said seriously, to reassure me. "The joint never changes, that's the beauty of it."

I shrugged.

"Everything you could ever want is right here—some beer, decent ratio, good ratio, some tunes... Or we could go an' change all the street signs around, play '*Confuse the new mailman*'. Come on, don't be such a Gloomy-Gus, a good ol' round a '*Confuse the new mailman*'. We just got this new one, and man, you should see this hummer. Let's go out an' change 'em all around again," he nodded down to his feet, thinking.

I was staring ahead, just standing there thinking about our futures. Were they in here? Was this the rest of our lives? Was this all there was?

He looked up, out in the direction I was, into all the people, "Well, sure, some of 'em are kind of ... some of 'em are kind of quiet... but to each his own, ya know. Stop thinkin' so much— come on, go with the flow, lighten up."

Suddenly, out of the crowd—"What 'er you jack-offs doin' back out here? Did I say you could come out here?"

"Hey Marty."

"Yeah Mar-tay, we filled out all the paper work... In triplicate."

"You pig-fuckers wanna fight?"

"Hey why don't cha go out 'n do the world a big ol' favor an' go fuck yerself," Jess pointed with his beer.

"Yeah, you should talk Jesster, you'd fuck a crack in the sidewalk." Marty was still trying to squeeze through the crowd to get to us.

Jess shrugged, "I fucked yer mother."

"Yeah, well, I fucked yer father, the horny son-bitch." He stood before us, but looked back through the crowd to where he was a few seconds before. "Ah go fuck yerself," he said to someone. "Go fuck yer mother."

Jess rolled his eyes.

Marty turned around. "Oh, party, man. Party party party..." he explained with his hands spread apart as if he were presenting us an invisible brick of gold. "...later ... at Leslie's," he brought his hands up to his chest as if to indicate big breasts, as he turned away.

I was hoping he wouldn't've come over to us, the big stooge, and luckily someone further back yelled something and his big head slowly rolled around. "Hey dick-scab... Yeah you, ya puss drippin' rag..." And he staggered away without saying anything more.

"Maybe Jen 'll be there," Jess shrugged as we watched Marty push his way through the crowd.

"Maybe," I shook my head a little, not believing it possible.

We sipped our beers and let them swing down to our sides, raising them and swinging them down like golden pendulums.

"Man, I loved her ... like nobody's business... I used to ask 'er to do shit all the time, but not once did she... I couldn't't've loved her more. I didn't think it was possible to feel that way." I felt light and floating around her—panicked even. And I felt weighed down and heavy when she wasn't around.

"So? ... You ever tell her how ya feel?"

"That shit never works... Me talking to anyone about that shit would be like me talkin' to a dog ... about dog food."

"What about that Terri girl?"

"Naw," I looked down and kind of shook my head a little. "She could never make up her mind about us. I'd get done talking with her and my head would be spinning. Felt like a whirlwind in my head... I need someone who makes me feel calm."

"I hate that, when Bettys plays all coy and all. Like we're supposed to read their minds."

"Yeah, to me that's the difference between bein' a little girl and bein' a woman—bein' honest about that shit, not playin' games."

"I hate that..." Jess shook his head. At first I thought he was talking about the Jen situation. He gestured ahead with his beer. "...All the dorks from our class are out partying like they're so hip 'n cool now, those gutless cowards..." he took a step forward. "...Yeah, you're so free!" he yelled. "You're so damn freakin' free... You're so god-damn in touch!"

I thought he was gettin' lit up, that he must've been drinkin' before he even picked me up. He turned to me and shook his head. He turned and shook his head in disapproval at no one in particular. "And all the partiers finally saw the light an' 'r at home studying," he looked back into the crowd. "Just look at 'em!" he yelled. He shook is head then snapped back to me. "Party?"

"Yeah... Why not," I exhaled.

Jess let his arm swing up for that last swallow, let his arm swing back down to his side and then as it swung back up, he let the bottle go and it sailed up into the air. It rose softly, hung in the air, caught all the dim lights, hung there as it glowed a golden flash in the darkness, then slowly began to drop...

He turned and rolled away, out the back door. I stood there for a second, the crowd all blending together. Then Jess yelled, "Come on," and I spun out into the back parking lot.

It was a lot cooler out now. My breath fogged in the air. Everything was still black, everything fading into the deep blank distance—the trees and trucks fading a dark gray. The gravel crunched under my Chuck Taylor high-tops. I could hear someone barfing behind one of the pickups. "I'm really tired man," I said as we walked. "So if I'm crabby or out-of-it, I'm just... It's just been a really weird week, a long way back and all." The fields were all bare, no golden grass, no golden sunshine like the summer out here. Everything was pressed flat in the darkness, like paper dolls.

"That's OK, man," he whacked my arm.

"I'm just adjusting to the..."

"What adjusting ... it's all the same, man. It's always the same. That's the truth, man, the hidden beauty."

That statement really stung me. It felt all heavy inside. I felt it sitting there, trying to turn inside of me, trying to turn me one way or another, but it couldn't. It just sat slumped in there, trying to hold me down. I twisted the bus ticket in my jacket pocket. "Anyway, thanks fer pickin' me up."

"Oh, no problem, man... That bus station's really freaky though," he reached for the door. "Lotsa weirdoes."

"Yeah," I muttered, even though the people there all looked the same to me.

The old truck rattled old noises—lost, forgotten and invisible, a symphony of many quiet little rattles.

Everything was so dark, as if not to ever exist again. There was no distance. No beginnings and no ends. Finally we passed a few people walking by the side of the road. "Hey, there's Lloyd—that Lumpkin kid." Jess looked up into the rear view mirror. "Lookit that freak. What say we get out 'n mess with 'im?"

"Naw... I don't feel like it. I'm gettin' too old fer that shit."

"Man..." he continued to watch him. "Were we ever that young?"

"It all feels so long ago..."

"Geees. Stop sayin' that shit, you're creepin' me out, man."

"All I remember was havin' a hard-on for like three years solid." I was looking back at them in the rear view mirror. They got smaller and smaller until they dissipated into the darkness, until they became that darkness.

"A constant woodrow, huh? You?"

"Yeah, like three years running, unrelenting. I don't think much blood was gettin' up to my brain. No oxygen 'r nothin' 'cause it was all puddlin' down there."

He looked over to me... "Cool." And we disappeared into the blank emptiness of ... and I thought about being here so long ago, how that blackness filled me, held me in place like an anxious solid, and how it filled me to overflowing and I'd do anything to empty some of it out, girls and drinking and yelling and running all around. But now it all seemed so empty, it all looked so blank and felt so cold, like there was nothing there at all, like it was all gone, like there was nothing left for anyone.

And finally Jess said, "So you're just tryin' ta figure it all out, huh?"

"Before I die."

"You think Danny had it all figured out?"

"I think he had things pretty well sorted out for himself. But everyone's different... I don't think he ever wanted that much."

"Some people never figure out what they want."

A young couple was stepping out of the weeds at the side

of the road. Their hair was all messed up, their clothes kind of sideways. They were holding hands, struggling up, pulling themselves from the ditch. We slowed to a stop next to them as I rolled down the window.

"Everything all right?" Jess leaned over to see who it was.

"Yeah, we're fine," the guy nodded. The girl looked away shyly, down the road behind us.

"All right," I shrugged and nodded, "Just checkin'," and we lurched forward and I rolled the window back up. "Jeez, the later it gets, the younger and younger the people seem to get."

We burrowed and floated, the darkness was not like that old solid: full and heavy to anchor you down, keep you in place, quiet, familiar, warm. Not like it had been at one time. It was as if it had been gone for so long now that it was hard to remember what it once was, how it felt to be out here late into the night with all the crisp weeds and that dark, flat dirt, all the fields as dark as the sky, the sky slamming down into the distance, the fields rising up, rushing out to become the sky, and us rushing along in the wind.

We slowed down a long, sandy driveway. Some of them are endless out here. They seem to go on forever. Old cars and pickups lined both sides. It was cold as we walked past them. A couple of the windows were fogged up, as if couples were making out in them. You could see some tiny dashboard lights trying their best to glow in the mist inside. And you could see a couple of little stars so far away, trying their best to be tiny hallows of light through the flat gray veil of cloud.

"Whadda you thinka that war?" Jess shivered as he huddled in his jean jacket, wrapping it tightly around himself with his hands in the pockets. The cars blocked some of the wind, but there were hardly any trees this far out, just the gusts of wind from the empty fields.

"Let's get it over with as fast as possible. I guess that's my feeling to just about everything right now."

We stepped up onto the tilting wood porch. The paint was half peeled away, kissed away in breaths of wind. And some faded gray person muttered, "Who's that?" to someone else in the darkness as they considered my little assessment. "Who cares," was the quiet reply as Jess stepped to the door.

A couple of people huddled here and there on the porch. They had their hands in their pockets, tightly wrapping their jackets around themselves. We nodded at some of them as Jess reached for the creaking screen door. I didn't recognized any of them.

It was pretty crowded inside the small old house. Not as crowded as the bar, but crowded enough. That Shooting Star song "Are You Ready" thumped from another room. Some beers were sitting on a rickety card table. We each grabbed one as we walked past. "I wonder if your little Jen-Jen 'll be here." Jess looked about mischievously.

"Doubt it," I coughed and cleared my throat.

We made our way through packs of people as we burrowed into the dimly lit house. That UFO song "We Belong to the Night" began sputtering as we tunneled deeper. A string of people were headed our way through the crowd, so we had to squeeze past some others and lean up against a wall to let the string pass. We leaned at the end of the long living room, right by the door into the dining room or kitchen, I couldn't tell which.

"It's funny..." I said.

"What?"

"Well, it's just so empty out here, without any of the grain or stalks of corn..." I held my beer in tight against the crowd.

"Hey isn't that? ...Aw, no. That ain't her."

"...and in here ... it's like a fuckin'..."

"Oh, hey, how's your brother and all?"

"Oh... You know... We don't really talk all that much. We don't got nuthin' much in common."

"Yeah, that's too bad, but family shit, it's weird shit and all, but it's always gonna be there. Some families just need time ta grow into one another."

"Or get as far away as they can from one another."

Some girl I didn't recognize walked past and flipped Jess off. "Oh I bet that's not what you do with that finger," he called as she was swallowed by the people in the other room.

"What's with her?"

He shook his head and crinkled his nose. "She's a stain, man. A real fuck stain. A real bone-brain."

Some people on the other side of the room were gesturing over to us as they talked amongst themselves. I swear I thought I heard one of them say "Dirt poor grubs" in reference to us.

I shook my head. "Man, they're kind of mean about all a..."

"Ah, they just don't know any better," Jess swung his beer up to his lips, held it there for a moment, then dropped it back down. The bottle caught the light inside of itself and glowed a thick, rich golden butterscotch for a moment. "They don't know how lucky they are. That's that Kenner crowd," he nodded. "See that guy, that guy there, he's on the tennis team. So what would you expect? Man, people like that don't even realize how lucky they are. All they ever have to do is just show up, just snap their fingers an' everything's right there for 'em. They ain't got nothin' ta worry about. Good things just come rushin' to them," he sort of shook his head. "All's they ever have ta do is just *show up.*"

I wanted to change the subject, change it all to something more golden, more permanent. "Remember that fort?" Just about every summer when we were in grade school we'd build a fort out in the wooded swamp back in the ravine behind my house. It was called "Jackson's Swamp" because it was out in this little ravine behind the Jackson's house. Really, the house was just this pathetic tarpaper shack with this huge garage next to it. That family spent all their money on cars. Hell, they spent all their time on cars. To each his own, though, I guess.

Anyway, we'd build these elaborate, multi-leveled forts in

the tall trees out in this wooded swamp. And we'd have to paddle out to them on styrofoam rafts that some kid got down at a motorcycle place. The large styrofoam slabs were from the motorcycle crates. I couldn't even imagine how that kid could get them all the way out there on his bike by himself.

Anyway, that was about the best time of my life, to have a little hideaway like that up in the clouds, where all my friends could hang out. "Those forts. Remember those forts? Damn, I miss those forts."

"Ah, there's good days ahead. It's easy ta romanticize the past... I mean don't get me wrong, those forts down by the river were cool an' all. Those were good times," Jess was searching into the crowd and not really concentrating on me. "That Kenner crowd, ppfff. What're they doin' out here? ... Hey, she's kinda cute. A tennis player," his eyes lit up and he smiled.

"Yeah, I know, but I meant the ones out in the swamp." He was thinking of forts on the banks of the river from high school in the fall and winter. We'd dig down into the ground, roll logs up and secure them together with wire and mud. Then we'd get plywood from the "midnight lumber yard"—any old construction site would do. We'd plywood the floor and walls on the inside and cover the outside with other logs and branches and mud and sod and leaves. You'd walk right past them if you didn't know where to look.

We'd carpet the inside—steal carpet outta neighbors' garages and throw in old stoves we'd raid from ice fishing houses. They were cozy little hide-a-ways—places to smoke and drink; look at cheaply made black and white magazines with titles like *Hot poppin' mamas* and bring girls to.

"Huh?"

"Those forts we'd paddle out to..."

"Not in this life we didn't."

"Yeah, remember..."

A girl staggered into the room trying to balance a TV tray and some beers in her arms. Another girl ran past crying. She hid her face in her hands.

Jess bent down to help unfold the tray. "Man, these thing's 'r real death traps," he said to her as he fiddled, then straightened up and turned back around to me.

"The forts," I said.

"Yeah," he sighed. "...I don't know if I'm ready to talk about him just yet. He's not out of my mind in that way. Maybe tomorrow, after I see he's really gone."

"Yeah."

"Hey, monkey-butt ... how 'bout her. She do anything for ya?" Jess nodded over to a crowd, but I knew which one he was thinking of, I could just tell.

"Yeah, she makes me happy ... nervous ... excited, scared, confused, tense, anxious... She's way outta my league. What about her," I nodded over to a younger girl I had my eye on since we arrived.

"I guess, but how do ya really know, nothing ventured, nothing gained," he was still thinking of the first girl he mentioned.

"You're so lucky, you don't get nervous." I was still glancing over now and then to the other girl to see if she was with anyone, hanging out with a specific guy—seems all the girls I like always end up being with other guys.

"You're so lucky. I always just end up pushing them away. Maybe it's a different kind of nervous, a reverse nervous."

"Yeah, I know what you mean. I hate that when shit gets screwed up between some Betty and me. I mean whadda ya do about it? Ya try an' talk to 'em an' it don't matter what ya say. No matter what ya say they're gonna be stinkin' pissed at ya. Talkin' only makes it worse. It just don't matter."

"Yep. You can always count on that one."

I was still looking at the younger girl. A little blond with short blond hair that shone in the smoky light. She was wearing an old high school letter jacket, the kind from the 60s, the kind with the leather sleeves. This one was gold with black sleeves, ripped and faded. And she wore faded jeans.

"You can forget that other one," Jess said. "She's nothin'

but trouble... Hey, see that guy. That guy there, right there," Jess whispered at me without looking at the guy or calling attention to ourselves. "His sister was the one from Central who killed herself after those hockey jock-holes made her take off her clothes and threw mud at her... Two summers ago... Out in the fields behind Central. She was just walkin' home ... and those dinosaurs happened along... And that other guy, over there," he nudged me with his elbow, "His brother went to Northside, just flipped out one day. Went ape-shit, hey. Yeah, they finally found him naked in a janitor's closet..."

"That guy?"

"Naw, his brother, man."

"He was with someone?"

"Naw, he was alone..." he tugged a swig of beer.

"He was goin' ta town on himself? Just a strummin' on the ol' banjo? Just pluckin' and a grinnin'?"

"No man, I guess he just snapped. Couldn't take it any-more—they found 'im stark raving naked, just wigged out, freaked. Found 'im curled up in a corner. He'd smeared his own shit on the wall an' all over himself. They had ta drag 'im outta there. An' word got around and everyone was really bummed about it—even the insecure hate mongers, fuckers who're always startin' shit, startin' shit storms... Yeah, he was on the football team an' everything. Man, he seemed to have it all. He had it made, hey."

"Stress," I offered cheerfully. "Anyway who'd wanna hang out with a bunch a Northsiders ... bunch a shallow, phony, trendy posers—sittin' around, bein' so clever, such a chore ta listen to..."

"Yeah, that stress 'll get ta ya there, boy. God only knows how long he'd been doin' that shit. No lie, pal." Jess looked around. "Damn, I wish I could be that uninhibited ... be that free."

"No shit," I laughed. "But isn't that what we're all doin' anyway, sortin' through our own b.s. In our own ways?"

"Why do I get the feeling all those jerks, all those over-competitive jocks, all those narrow minded rednecks, all those over-compensating posers are gonna be out there in ten years tryin' ta sell me insurance, metal siding, shit like that."

"Probably," I shrugged.

"Ah, maybe they'll wise up by then. God only knows where that poor kid is now. The family was so embarrassed they sent him away to some relatives in Chicago or something, you know, to let the guilt really sink in. Seems a bunch a kids were pickin' on 'im. You know those insecure hate mongers—when they're not bein' mean, they're bein' stupid. And when they're not bein' mean *or* stupid, they're bein' mean *and* stupid."

"Yeah but that shit happens ta everybody... I mean, I could give two shits about what all the self-centered little Hitlers out there have ta say about me, tryin' ta make themselves important by always rippin' everyone else down. Where's that gonna get ya? What've they ever done?"

Jess shrugged and raised his eyebrows, as if saying, "Hey, some guys are sensitive, let things get to them." He grabbed a beer from someone passing by. "You have two shits?"

"Yeah, but I'm saving one for later," I nodded, "Hey, who knows, sometimes a guy's just gotta roll around in his own poo," I shrugged.

"Yeah, sometimes it's all I can do not to just wear my own poop all over myself."

"Surely."

"Speaking of which... I gotta piss."

When Jess got back I was in the kitchen, sort of crouching down, looking at this old toaster. The thing curved almost like a chrome bowling ball. It was like something from another world, from another time. The world reflected around it, curving, twisting, rolling, flowing, stretching to separate into individual colors, strands of colors bending around in lines, the world rushing in thin strings of color, flowing in currents, like magic.

"Trying to find yourself," Jess grabbed the back of my collar with one hand and pulled me up. As I stood I faced a window that was open. Someone was passing beers through to people out on the back porch. But I really didn't notice them, I just stared out into the infinite, endless flat fields of dirt and sky.

Jess was drinking a different beer now. He was swaying and slurring his words a little. "Why you gotta be wearin' new clothes?" he leaned in to me to steady himself. He seemed serious.

"Sometimes I feel so weird. So light, like maybe I don't really belong out here, like I don't really belong anywhere," I stared into the darkness, the blankness, "Like everything's changing and I'm just staying the same. Or everything's the same and I'm changing... It doesn't really feel like he's gone. I mean, this place seems so different now, so distant, so remote. But... Man, I thought he'd always be out here—always be a piece of this place—a piece of my life..."

"He is a part of your life. And you were meant to be here, my man. Or wait. No. No. That's not it, none of us were meant to be here. In fact, none of us *are* here, we're not here at all, we're all somewhere else..." Jess was gesturing wildly, stepping backwards without looking, mocking me.

"No, no. It's like a mistake has been made..."

"Are you kidding. You've been up for, like, a week straight... Finals, the bus ride up here. Whadda ya expect ta feel like? Besides, this place is heaven. Man-up, pal. Just look at it," he stepped up to the window and stood right next to me. "Everything's right here," he raised one of his arms to stress the point and illustrate how vast this place was, its potential. "Hey if you don't like it here, then fuck you too, pal—'cause I'm stayin'. Just look at all this room. All of this space. It's all for us."

"I didn't mean it that way, it's a nice place an' all, it's just sometimes I get this feeling that I'm..."

"Feeeeeelinnnnngggs, nothing more then fffffeeeeeellli- innnngggsss," he broke into song and slowly began gesturing and spinning, bumping into people passing through.

I turned to watch him, and right as I turned a fist came right at me. It all happened so suddenly, yet it was as if in slow motion.

Out of the blue a fist whizzed to my head like a rocket, landed in the middle of my face, knocked me back, off my feet, the room spun, colors smeared to lines, I wasn't expecting it, the floor was wet with beer and sand and mud, I slid right back, just slipped right to the ... I snapped up and shook my head as I sat up on the wet ... the strings of colors forming blobs and slabs, then a foggy haze, then shadows and outlines emerged to the surface, bringing definition, and just as I looked back up I saw Marty pummeling some guy I'd never even seen before.

"...sack of fuck." Big Marty already had him laid out on the floor in the corner and was now stepping up to stomp on the guy's ribs. Just as he was raising his foot, some people quickly snatched me up from the floor. They raised me by my arms and were helping to brush me off when I saw Marty turning and walking to me. He turned his head around to look back at the guy in disgust, then turned back to me as he approached.

"You OK?" he nodded.

"Yeah, I guess," I was brushing myself off. "Thanks."

"No worries, man. What was that all about?"

"You tell me. I never even..."

"Oh, that's just Petey; he's always just so, well, you know." It was that short blond girl I'd been watching. She was at my side holding my arm up. She was talking and talking to me, but I really didn't make out any of her words. I was just so stunned from the sudden unexpected punch and slipping and confusion and then I couldn't believe she was here, that she was at my side, right next to me, talking to me, it was all such a whirl, a...

"...Petey-pie, he's just so jealous and protective. I think it's his way of showing off or something. I think he'll grow outta it though. Or I hope he will. I mean, you never really know, he gets kinda keyed up about everything. I think he needs a hobby, keep his mind occupied," she was talking and talking, but I didn't really hear her. I just couldn't believe she was right there, so close to me, actually touching me, helping me, as if I mattered to her, my head was spinning in a weird fog and everything was hard to process, some colors were brighter than others, then I could only see *her*, and everything else was moving slowly, receding into the background and dimming.

"Yeah, I'm fine, thanks," I was looking right at her. I couldn't take my eyes off of her. She was like a soft feathery magnet flame with short blond hair, permanent smile, old gold sweater, fading soft blue jeans...

"You OK, big guy?" Jess had my other arm.

"Yeah," I nodded.

"Well alrighty then," and he stepped away to leave us alone, walking to the corner and grabbing the guy who slugged me and he and some others dragged him around the corner into the other room.

"This is really stooooopid," she said. "My name is Wendy," she held out her small hand.

"Ah, yeah. Hi," I shook it and didn't let go, but it sort of slipped down, so I tugged the bottom of her jacket and softly pulled her over to the wall and positioned myself against the wall for some good, solid lean time.

Some other people were stepping in the room to see what happened, and she raised her hand up over to them, as if to say everything was all right, not to worry, everything was cool.

After a while I asked her outside where it was more quiet, where we could talk without being interrupted, where we could be alone. We were sitting on the steps of the back porch, sitting right up next to one another against the crisp night. I kept forgetting her name and she just laughed at this, that little laugh of hers. "Where's your head tonight?" she wondered as she laughed and shook her head and gazed out into the black fields. She pulled a pen from her jacket and took my hand and set it in her lap and began writing on my palm.

"You writing your name so I'll remember? So I'll always have it? You giving it to me ... so people will call me Wendy from now on?" I didn't want to stare into those fields anymore. I just wanted to look at her.

"Of course," she was leaning down, into my hand "...and I'm writing you a little poem." That was the thing with girls like that, they could make you new again. They knew how to make everything new again.

"How ya like the big city? Is it exciting?"

I drew in a deep breath. "Yeah, it's not bad. It's exciting, and it's alienating in a way. It's hard to meet people, and everyone's just out for themselves. Not like out here."

"So, what's a 'cowboy'? I heard my brother call people that before, but he'd never tell me what it meant." She was only a few years younger than me, but in a way she seemed younger and older at the same time, like she was from another age, like she knew different things, like she was from another place, or another time, another world. She knew things I didn't know about—girl things.

"Oh, that. That's nothin'. A cowboy's just a coward. A follower. It's funny, the way different people talk, depending on when and where you grew up—what's insulting, what's a compliment—perceptions, expectations."

"What's a 'spy'?" she was holding my fingers now. She was so warm and soft and I leaned in closer to hear her, to breathe in her breaths.

"A spy's just a quiet person, that's all. You know, that quiet guy who always sits alone, reading in the back of class. They're the ones who always seem to end up overthrowing the government ... or inventing something really cool."

"What's a 'shiny penny'?"

"Oh, you know, some phony who talks a lot but never does anything. Thinks they know everything. A pretender. Boastful, but worthless. Someone who's flashy and braggy and gossipy, talks all the time, bla bla bla, but unoriginal. Just a Xerox copy. All shine but not worth anything. Like someone who drives a fancy car and wears expensive clothes just to impress people."

"So, what 'r you?"

"Oh me? I'm a 'cowboy spy'. A 'shiny cowboy spy'."

"Eeemm, no you're not," she looked up at me and shook her head. "Do you ever wonder who invented the 'spork'?"

"Spork?"

"Yeah, we were at Kentucky Fried Chicken before we came out here, the one by the interstate, an' you know, one of those plastic spoon-fork things. A 'spork'."

"Oh, those things. Yeah, I wonder about them all the time. In fact, I'm in therapy for obsessing about them. Can't get anything else done. It's been haunting me for the longest time... What would make you think of that?"

She laughed, then shrugged, "What would make me think of anything? ... So how do you know Marty from?"

"From bein' around. School I guess." I really wasn't sure if I wanted to be associated with him or not. I guess he was my friend and all, but he was such an obnoxious loudmouth, you never knew how someone was going to take him. "Don't believe everything you hear about a guy... I'm not a Nazi and I've never burned down any orphanages full of sightless children. I've had better things to do."

"Oh, I know how it goes. I know all about that stuff. Liars and salesmen are all over the place—always tryin' ta ruin stuff... Petey back there, you can't believe a thing he says. And Marty's never mentioned you."

"Why? How'd you know him?"

"I've known him for a while now," she leaned in to examine my shoes.

"From parties," I nodded.

"From him being my brother," she nodded.

"Oh, yeah, that whole deal. With Becky and that other Becky," I nodded to myself.

"Stella," she smiled, "Stella's between me and Becky."

I was surprised. I could hardly say anything. I never pictured Marty with a family, much less a sister who'd actually be quiet and thoughtful and peaceful and so at ease with everything, and certainly not someone as delicate as her. And I couldn't picture her with a family like his, I could only picture her in a middle-class rambler in an old suburb. Bright green lawn. Boat in the backyard. Chain-link fence for the collie. Sitting up on the roof in the middle of the night with her friends, listening to music from a little radio, sneaking cigarettes after a party, looking up into the starry sky and all its secrets. A little cabin she'd go up to on weekends in the summer. Her and her friends would go up there and have campfires and water ski. They'd go out to the bars at night and hang out with the other middle-class cabiners their age. And the cabin would be up a hill, surrounded by tall trees, a winding path down to the dock, a great view of the lake. And she'd party up there with her friends in college, and she'd lose her virginity up there. "Gosh I never thought of..." I whispered.

"My parents are divorced an' everything. I live with my mom in the city. She's remarried."

"Either way, he might bust me up good if he knew we were out here together." I was looking back, to the back door.

"So we're 'out here together', huh?"

"We seem to be." I rubbed her back with my palm, warming her, slid it up to her shoulders, put my arm around her, slowly drew her to me, leaning in to kiss her. She tasted so fresh and new.

"So, you know many girls? Back in the city?" she drew in a breath after our kiss.

"Oh. No ... not me. I know some girls and all, but nobody nice. How 'bout you?"

"No, the guys around here are just... I don't know... They're all too busy trying to impress each other. Stumbling over each other. It's really lame. I guess I just know them all too well, growing up together and all, it would just be weird..."

"Yeah, I know what you mean. A lot of my friends think it's the absolute end of the world if you don't have a girlfriend. It's all they ever concentrate on."

"Yeah, there's definitely more to life than just that. Most of the guys in my mom's neighborhood are too focused on wasting their time with video games... Maybe it's just a matter of meeting the right person ... at the right time... It's a timing thing." We kissed again. Her mouth was so warm and her breath was thick with beer and smoke. "What're you studying?" she was smiling as I pulled away.

"...Oh, I'm in literature right now," I couldn't take my eyes off of her, but thought she might think I was a complete goofball if I just stared at her like that, so I looked down at my feet.

"Reading it ... or writing it?"

"Just reading right now... But I was thinking of getting into journalism ... or something like that," I shrugged. "I hope that doesn't sound pretentious or anything."

"To be a newspaper reporter, that's kinda cool. It'd be really interesting meeting so many different stories. It'd be a good variety."

"Eeemm. I don't know. Reporting seems like a real weasely thing though. They always need to know everything ... in that nosy way. They never see five minutes in front of their own eyes. Where journalists are ... they're more like ... well, they seem to be three days ahead of everyone else. Kind of hanging back a little an' just commenting on things."

"Like a cowboy spy."

"Maybe," I smiled and nodded in considering this "...Journalism just seems more permanent somehow. Reporting seems too temporary, just throwing stories away one after the other."

"I don't know, that seems like the hardest thing—to figure out what to be. I mean, not that I'm worried about it, it's just so huge to think about sometimes... Maybe you could write for a cool magazine?"

"Yeah, maybe ... but on the other hand, I don't need no magazine telling me what to think or feel, like some phony poser, so why should I impose on others? ... Sometimes I get this weird sense of loss when I think about the future. Like I'm losing my past or something."

"I don't know, I wouldn't mind losing my past sometimes. Start all over. See new things. Not that I'm ashamed of anything, it's just the future's so much bigger and better, more adventurous ... think of everything that's out there. Think of all the good stuff that's waiting out there for you... Maybe it's a good thing to break away from your past, in order to find your future. Think of what you'll have in, like, five years."

"Emm... It's hard though... the past is so safe." I was looking right into her blue eyes. "I'm not perfect you know... I mean, I'm just as hairy and smelly and lazy as any other guy..."

"I like my guys hairy and stinky. Super extra hairy. Extra stink too."

"All of 'em?"

"Yep. All thirty of 'em... But I like you just the way you are."

Our arms were rubbing against each others and after a while we began comparing arms—length and shape, color and complexion, hair length and density. We compared moles. I started counting mine. "I call them Wendys," I whispered and she smiled, "So you'll always be living all over me."

I leaned in and kissed her again. And she looked up and put her hands over her heart and whispered, "I'll never brush my teeth again," and laughed. Then she looked down into her soft, warm hands and then back up to me.

"You're friends with that one guy, huh?" she asked when we were lying together on an old ratty couch upstairs. It was pitch black up there and warm and the party murmured downstairs. It was a nice feeling—to have them all there—but not so near. I had my arms around her and she had her arms around me and our legs were entangled and she was so warm and soft and smelt so full, so fresh and new and clean, like the crisp fall wind outside, like the dry leaves and the moist fields and everything.

"You should've seen this fort we built. Man, you should've seen us together... But somehow things changed," I said between kisses and breaths. "Do you believe in ghosts?" We were lying together, curled up into one another.

"I believe in singing ghosts. How 'bout that," she whispered. She was kissing me now, not the quick short porch-type kisses, but the deep long kisses that turned you inside out.

"We should go back downstairs," I whispered, "Your brother will be looking for you... I wouldn't want to upset him."

"He won't care," she whispered. "Do you know many girls? ... I mean, back in the city?"

"A few... But not like this."

"Oh."

"Would you come with me tomorrow. It'd mean a lot to me... I think he'd like that. To see us together." Our eyes were closed and our mouths were breathing in one another, drawing in one another's breath, searching into one another.

"Yeah... I'd like that."

"I'll never see him again."

"God musta needed another angel up in heaven then... And he'll always be around..." she closed her eyes "...It's good to have a lot to remember..."

"Those days are gone..."

"So you can have more days... More days to come..."

wooden horses

He slowed his Mercedes in front of the garage, stopping beside the neighbor's rusted-out pickup. The beat-up truck was parked sideways in the drive on the other side of the dilapidated fence.

The driveway was next to the house, so with only a step or two he was in the back entry. Slowly he lowered himself onto the corner of a wooden chair. His briefcase met the floor and his arms settled on the armrests. The back entry smelled moist and full as he closed his eyes and leaned forward into the thick spring breeze. He was relieved to be home.

The wind had ripened the entry with freshness that evening, but the back was generally too musty on most others. The room looked as though it had been an open porch at one time, but had been closed in some time ago and didn't get that clean cross ventilation that you'd want.

The chair was a rickety lawn chair found upside down in the mud of the backyard when they moved in. It was the only thing in the long, narrow back room. He couldn't recall how or when the chair had found its way in from the lawn, and wondered why they never found the time to get more of them as they had always talked about.

He was looking out into the yard when his wife stepped in from the kitchen. The yard was plain and simple, with a dry patch of soil in front of a little wooden gazebo. The circular gazebo had just enough room for two. It had weathered gray as the paint wore off. It stood tilted as it was when they moved in, like a hood ornament from an old car that had never been in fashion. He'd been talking about cleaning it up ever since.

Several weeds spotted the dirt around it, but it was still in pretty good shape. It just needed to be tidied up some, that was about all. Basically just a coat of paint, maybe a nail or two, that's about all. He says it will make the back look not so mangy. That and some fertilizer, maybe trim back the bushes. But it was all in pretty good shape. That was how he saw it.

"How'd it go?" she sang. She looked down at the plate she was wiping, her hand circling it slowly with a small dish towel, her face reflected in its shine.

He leaned back into the chair. "It went fine," he said, cocking his head to the side, blowing the day out from his mouth as he loosened his tie.

She smiled and rubbed the plate a bit slower.

He was still gazing out at the gazebo and whistling through his teeth.

"See," she said.

She was excited about the little gazebo when they were shown the place. It was weathered a sort of gray that matched the picket fence and garage and house. She thought it would make a nice little dining spot, and he agreed as they drove off. She liked the sense of enclosure here, the sense of closeness. The houses were all very close, plain two stories with long thin slits for backyards. The area was stuffed with them, the yards overgrown with trees. It was all so warm and cozy, and everything was in pretty good shape.

The fence around the yard was like the rotting bones of an animal that had collapsed there ages ago. The bones were ragged and fraying with sleep. They ached as the wind breathed through them. The garage was leaning like a tent. The door forever agape because the stiff garage door couldn't fold down due to the angle of the garage's lean. It needed a new roof and everything could've used some paint. The house wasn't that bad either—the basement leaked from time to time and the place could use a rewiring job, maybe new plumbing, but things were in pretty good shape there, too.

"Good to be home," he finally said.

"It's late, and you must be hungry, so how 'bout some sup—it's on me," she disappeared into the kitchen.

"Free supper, my favorite kind," he smiled, then went upstairs to change.

After dinner he sat at their small dinner table between the back entry and the kitchen. The TV was on the table, flickering a fraying black and white that barely held the picture. He wasn't paying much attention, something about clear cutting forests. There was a fuzzy picture of a mountain stubbled with stumps. "Man, I'm getting sick of this station—nuthin' but depressing stuff," he was looking back through the kitchen, into the yard, remembering that night it stormed the first week and they had to sleep in the back entry as their bedroom in the attic leaked so bad. He looked over his shoulder to her. She was standing in the middle of the kitchen, looking down at something in her hands. She examined it closely, rubbed it in a towel, then looked at it again. She let go and it dropped into a grocery bag at her feet.

He spun off his chair and walked to the middle of the room. The walls were bare and there was hardly any furniture. The sun was setting and it cast cloudy orange shadows though the windows onto the walls. He stood looking down at the wood floor for a quiet moment, then he bent down and picked a piece of lint from the floor. He turned and stepped into the kitchen and stood across from her in front of the bag. He looked down and let the toothpick he had been sucking and the lint he was holding drop into the bag. "What's that?" he asked.

She was looking down into the bag as well. "Just a fork with a tooth missing." She looked up at him and made a face. He reached an arm down and snatched up the garbage in one motion. He stuck his tongue out at her, turned and walked out to the driveway.

Curtis Wait was in his backyard next door. He could just see Curtis' head above the peeling fence. He saw Curtis' head moving as he packed the bag into the can in front of the garage. It looked as though Curtis was wandering around, his head sort of bobbing about. Between a crack in the fence he could make out that pale, thin body through rips in Curtis' shirt, but he couldn't figure out what Curtis was doing.

When he walked back inside, she was leaning against the counter, rocking up on her toes to peer out the window and down into Curtis' backyard. His lawn was overgrown with bushes and weeds. "Come rumba with me" was painted on his bright yellow garage door in blazing red letters.

"What is it?" he asked, looking back at the table with his papers in front of a couple screaming and pointing at each other on the silent TV. The sepia and silver screen flickered a slight glow in the dim room. The sun was melting over the houses behind the ones across the street. The backyards were deep with lazy shadows, thousands of dark holes melting through into other places and other times.

"I think he's dancing again," she whispered with a smile, still leaning and stretching to unravel the mystery.

He cleared his throat and looked at the TV. "All he ever does is write and paint; he barely has enough to feed himself," he walked back to his table. "What he needs is someone to tell him when to mow that lawn. And that house..." he shook his head and muttered to himself. "A wasted life," he appraised. "Not that I'd ever tell *him* that, the crazy son-of-a-bitch. He'd probably sneak over in the middle of the night and burn our house down..."

"He's not dangerous... or crazy. Sounds like you're jealous, alpha male," she smiled and looked back, "destroying everything in your path, always looking for an angle," she laughed.

"Yeah, that'd be me," he smiled.

"That, I believe, is his 'Death Dance'."

"Is that so... To ward off death?"

"To embrace it... He says it's to acknowledge death as a state of being—death as a phase or passage, a stage you wait in until you are reborn again." She looked over to her husband. His head was down, concentrating on his work at the table, his fingers working a calculator, a pen in his mouth. "He thinks death would be like being in a shopping mall, like a giant waiting room—poisoned by the blind conformity of the 'adjusted'... Waiting to be re..."

"Least he's not doing his 'gloat' dance, from when he thought he'd won the lottery... I mean, here he is, this artist type, always hanging back, on the sidelines, commenting on society, but not in the game, supposed to be above material superficialities, and here he gets excited by a little money. Who does he think is buying his art? Construction workers? Office professionals? No, it's rich people. People with money, with discretionary..."

"Oh, I liked his gloat dance, very free and uninhibited, though I think it would've been more effective with clothing."

"Remember when the Smiths went on vacation and he painted each board on their house a different color? Damn, that thing looked like the end of the damn rainbow," he said through the pencil in his mouth.

"Their house was always too bland anyway, it needed a little color," she turned to watch Curtis skip and gallop around his backyard. And she thought about when she first met her husband, in dance class in college. He was the best dancer, his perfect back, slightly arched, perfect motion—fluid and flowing, like a robot following the instructor, mimicking old dances and now Curtis inventing his own, living life on his own terms.

Suddenly, through the spots of shadow and light, it struck her that Curtis looked like a paper doll or wooden horse she used to play with as a kid. She used to dance them on her knees on long car trips while up north hunting with her dad. And she thought about what had become of those galloping wooden horses. Maybe they're down in a box in her mother's basement. Maybe she could find them, dig them up, pull them out again, put them up on a shelf in their bedroom. "Waiting to be reborn," she whispered to herself.

Later they sat at the dinner table, she was curled with her legs folded up to her chest reading a book and he was working on his stuff. She looked out into the kitchen every now and then. He was busy and tired. The wind was cool through the windows and all the quiet little sounds settled themselves outside. It reminded her of those trips up north, her dad, long since gone, wanting nothing more then to 'catch' a deer, as he called it, although he didn't really catch one, he'd shoot at one from a distance. And she thought about standing there in the thick woods, admiring things from afar; about how 'wanting' always made her feel that possessing things somehow ruined them.

Nearly every night she reads a story aloud while they lie in bed. It helps them go to sleep. The light on her bed stand is a dim yellow. It slowly pulsates, just barely breathing, glowing on the wall as the faint gold of an old newspaper. He lies facing the wall away from her. After about twenty minutes of reading, she turns out the light.

She reads stories of clumsy, confused lives—a story a night. She lives those lives slowly. Sometimes she lies with the book on her chest for a few minutes, her arms lightly around it, letting it all sink in. His head is always turned away, his eyes closed, but he always can tell that hers are open, living those lives for just a moment, holding that book slightly, as if holding a child.

But that night she heard some rustling out back. She could hear Curtis rummaging through their garbage in the dark of the night's imagination. She could hear him pulling up that fork, holding it up in the moonlight to examine it for a moment. She could hear him pull himself up and back over the rickety fence. Looking back, she could see small lights pulsating, must be candles in his attic studio, burning into the night.

There was no story that night. He was warm and thought about tomorrow, going over things for a moment in his mind. He faced the wall and felt her lying next to him, but she was leaning against the window in the dark, looking down into Curtis' backyard, into the simmering glow of night, into its soft, velvety silence.

how I hope to die

I'm at work. At the record store. I need to write something, but I'm stuck. I can't think of anything super groovy. I need to turn something in for my weekly column in the free journal I write for. When stuck, the common advice always seems to be: write what you know, but I already know what I know, so writing about it would be redundant. Besides, I'm bored with what I know, bored staring at the same four walls all the time, bored staring at the same four walls in my mind. Maybe I just get bored easily. Maybe I should write about what I don't know. But I don't know what I don't know. So I think about that awhile—about all that I can't see, all that I can't know.

For inspiration and direction, I flip through the paper. I find random headlines and images can form a collage which then forms a storyline. Turning the pages, I come across the obituaries. Now I don't like to dwell on such details myself as I figure life is for living, not for worrying. Today has enough worries, never mind the troubles of tomorrow, which are plentiful in themselves.

Quickly I compose my own obituary in my notebook, what they'll probably say about me when I pass on—

He had a really clean apartment. He needed a couch, so that people would want to actually stay awhile. He wrote several stories that some people seemed to read at one time. He usually showed up on time, which would have been appreciated had more people noticed. He didn't dress all that badly. He talked to a girl he really liked once, but it didn't go any further than that. He tried real hard, but in the end I don't know that it really mattered all that much. Someone gave him a beer once and he seemed to really enjoy that. One time they promised him a hot dog, but then they didn't have any and he seemed real sad about that, but I think he was probably really actually upset about something else entirely, though he probably wasn't self aware or evolved enough to realize that.

Perhaps you can't sum someone up with just a few words. At my funeral, instead of a eulogy, I prefer a good, tight, twelve minute drum solo from Neil Peart, the drummer from the rock band Rush. I think that'd pretty much sum me up: a Neil Peart drum solo.

Scanning the obits I notice the way people die—car crash, plane falling out of the sky, sickness, suicide, overdose, just plain old fashioned keeling over or going to sleep and not waking up. You'd think they'd be able to prevent some of that nowadays. You'd think they'd be able to put off that big dirt nap for a while, give a guy a few more years to see things, do things. Well, at least that's one thing I don't know about—my own death. So I start writing about that—

I don't know anything about how it happens, or when or why I pass away. I have no idea about any of the details other than supposedly I'm going to be there at the time. So I guess I'll just have to speculate and embellish. If I had my druthers, at this point and time anyway, I picture my death unfolding as something like this—

"I'm walking down the sidewalk. I stop in front of an old used record store. A dilapidated one-story brick building on the unfashionable side of town. I go inside as it reminds me of a mellow place where I used to work when I was young and carefree. The place is dingy. Grainy dust hangs in the air. There are some old couches slumped about (on one a shaggy dropout is napping. On another a young woman has her eyes closed and is sobbing, her face a twist of contortion, several beer cans around her. She looks like she wants to be left alone). But the place is full of old records—bins and bins of them, and boxes and stacks under those, and piles and piles in the back room. There is a huge pile of old paperback books in the corner, old science fiction—novels, anthologies, story collections, you name it—people come in and lay on the old couches and read for awhile sometimes, as if to take a break from life. The place suddenly reminds me of my college days, time rushing up to me, reminding me of some of the people I used to know..."

The bell above the door gently jingles. Someone is here. I stop writing and look up. A potential costumer has entered. He stops and looks around. He's wearing the standard businessman attire—an ill-fitting suit and tragically out-of-style tie.

"What's back there?" he nods, as if looking for a lost child.

"Overstock," I shrug, looking back down to my notebook, "You're not missing out on anything."

The suit guy wanders in further, slowly winding through the aisles. Out of the corner of my eye I can tell he stops at the "T-U" section. He flips through some old albums, picking up a few to look them over, front and back. I figure he's going to put on some early Thin Lizzy. He seems like an early Thin Lizzy guy, has that vibe about him.

He pulls out an album, holds it above his head. "Can I play this?" he asks.

"On your left," I call without looking up.

Some of the side aisles have old record players, waiting on old end tables or stools so people can test potential purchases. The man walks over and stands before one for a moment as if he's thinking about dropping the needle on that record.

I glance up and hope he does. It's a wise move.

And finally he indulges. He puts the record on, then sits on the old couch next to the old end table. He sinks in, closes his eyes. He looks really really tired, as if tired of it all. The song begins. "Out in the Street", from an old UFO album (from the 1970s hard rock group), a bold move from a crafty veteran, and one who is clearly deeply in the know (there were a lot of 'out in the street' type songs in the mid to late 70s, and the above was one of the better).

Funniest thing—I get busy and forget about him. I get a

few phone calls, then start in jotting something else down, fill out some paperwork, order some things, file some stuff, send some emails, make a call, jot some more things down, some other strains of thought, and some others come in and mill about. Finally, it's the end of the day. I take my last walk around, straightening things until I'm standing in front of the guy. He doesn't move. The record's been over for at least an hour. Gently I kick the side of the guy's shoe, but there's no response. He looks pale. Doesn't seem to be breathing. I stand there for a moment, then lean to shout in his ear, "Hey *dumb-ass*! ... Wake up, my man! ... *Closin' time*! ... Go home! Come back tomorrow! We need your business!" but he doesn't even budge, so I stare at him for a moment, thinking that might be unsettling to him, maybe freak him out a little, get him uncomfortable enough to jostle a little or even get up, that whole 'someone-staring-at-you' thing. But he doesn't. So I lean in and start in with the whole: "Your mother's an ugly whore!" thing. But he doesn't wake up. So I crank it up a notch with the: "Your wife's an unsightly prostitute!... Your value system is corrupt and immoral!... Your wife smells like a monkey!" only shouting really loud now, like wake-up-the-entire-neighborhood loud. But that doesn't do it either, so I start yelling: "Monkey wife! ... Monkey wife! ... Hairy monkey wife!" But no response, so I draw up a big gulp of breath and scream: "Go back to your monkey wife, loser!!! ... Go back to your monkey stinking wife, monkey stinker!!!" super loud. I start hopping up and down, acting like a monkey myself, going "Oooo Oooo Ooo, Ahh ahh ahh," like a monkey, up and down, flailing my arms, frustrated at him, angry at him for taking up my time, for bothering me. And then I realize he has probably passed away peacefully right there on that couch, and that just makes me even more frustrated and angry at him for being dead, because now not only do I have to sort a bunch of old, scratchy disco records some super-loser brought in, but now I've got to deal with dead guy here. I start kicking the side of the couch and flailing my arms about in dramatic, windmill motions and screaming: "Get back to work, you lazy sack of chicken crap! ..." But soon I am out of breath and exasperated. I stand there heaving, only able to muster a slight wisp of a whisper now: "Go back to your loser monkey wife, your crap-heaving, stinking monkey life partner... Go back to all the gnats... The hairy beast... The monkey dung strewn about your living room... You like that, eh? ... Don't cha? ... Flinging that poo... Smearing it *aaaalllllll* over... The foul odor... The aroma... The hair... The thick, matted hair," I stare at him for a few seconds... He looks dead, sort of an unanimated, dull hue to him, like an old plastic doll... He didn't look peaceful, he just looks ... tired... I don't know, lost somehow. Like he'd been lost so long he couldn't find his way out of being lost so he just had to live in that lost state for years.

I guess I should feel bad about yelling at a dead guy, but I don't... I guess I'm still mad at him for being dead, for leaving us... I hope someone is going to miss him.

I turn around, but there is no one else in the store. Then I look out the window, to the street, hoping for someone with that magic life-saving ability which I just don't seem to possess.

Luckily the local constable is sauntering by, so heavy with life and knowing it.

I run to the window, slapping my palm on the glass. I point behind me and then wave the copper in. He nods, acknowledging me, and walks to the door. Strangely, there is someone in a car at the curb. That someone looks vaguely like me, but a younger version of me, as if there could be several versions of me out there. The me in the car slaps on the glass of the window with his palm, talking to me, but I can't understand what he's trying to communicate.

I peek out, the constable ambling up the walk. "Hey, hey, Doug. There's a guy in here," I call to the constable, then run back in.

Doug, the constable, walks past me, entering, sensing the weirdness in my voice, all warblely and strained (Doug comes in for free coffee just about every day, so we know him well enough).

I peek out again to stare at that car with the young version of me in it. Strangely, the car is like one I always wanted to have, but could never afford (not a new sports car or overly fancy conspicuous-consumption over-compensation competition mobile, but an older sports car—a Jaguar XKE in robin's egg blue, with shiny spoke hub covers and a wide white racing stripe).

Doug says something, breaking my concentration, snapping the hold the car and the other me have on my attention. I turn and wander back in.

I walk back to the impossibly old couch amongst the aisles of plywood record bins. We stand in front of the musty old couch, above the guy who's just slumped there with his eyes closed, as if he's just sleeping one off.

"I ... I think he's a goner," I stammer. "We ... We've never had a death in here... Honest," I wheeze, as if scared to get in trouble. "He came in and ... and sat down. Like two hours ago. And that was it. I forgot about him, honest. I been over there, working and writing ... all afternoon."

"Did you check his neck?" Doug asks.

"For what?" I lean in, looking at his neck.

"For a pulse," Doug looks the guy over.

I don't answer, as if my non-answer will signify a no.

"Welp," Doug the constable swallows, leans in, reaching for the guy's neck and holding his hand on it for a moment, then slowly retracting, "Looks like I'll have to call this one in," he sighs, as if it's interrupting some peaceful moment. He turns his head to the little microphone on his shoulder and begins talking official sounding constable words into it as he walks to the door.

I lean in to study the man. He looks very average. And pale. I can't tell if it's a death kind of pale, or just a regular average guy kind of pale. I see he's holding a small photo in his hand, an old one. I twist my neck around to see the photo. It's a girl who looks to be college age. The photo has to be at least twenty years old. Maybe twenty five or thirty. Must be an old girl friend or something. I lean back again and suddenly feel bad for the guy, like he's been carrying around this crush, this loss, this lost opportunity for years. Suddenly I feel like I'm intruding, so I give the man his peace. I put the record back in play and wander back to the front. Seems the least I could do for the poor guy.

They come and take him away, lifting the body that now acts like a giant wet noodle, flopping this way and that, sagging in the middle as they spread him out on a cart. His arm flops down like a rag doll, dangling to scrape against the old tile floor. His hand drags across the years of cracks, discoloration, and stains as they wheel him out. They flip his arm back onto his chest so casually as if to not comprehend that this was a full-on human only a few short moments ago.

They cart him away. And that's it for that guy.

I follow them out, curious as to what's going to happen. But nothing does happen. There is no magic or sadness or whatever, just the tired leftovers of the day lingering in the air. I lean against the doorjamb, watching as if I'm now somehow responsible for him. They load him into a nondescript van like a deflated loaf of stale bread and drive off, leaving me alone, watching the last of the day slip away. I look around. The light blue Jaguar XKE is gone, as if it appeared only momentarily—as if to remind me of something I'm missing out there, or something I'm going to miss in the future.

I stand around for a while, then realize I'm late for supper. I close up shop and walk off, to get some tacos at 'Nowhere', the local taco stand. It's not my usual taco night, but I figure I deserve some expensive food after ignoring a man while he died.

I walk around a while, in a kind of fog. The death has seemed to change things for me. Everything seems to move real slow now. The clouds seem lower, grayer.

When I open up again, the night crew is already there. I walk inside and stand there. Tommy and Doris are behind the counter.

"Where'd you go?" Tommy asks, wondering where I'd

been.

"'Nowhere'," I stop and stare, aware of the death again, as if his absence were a presence in the room, "Just got back from 'Nowhere' again," I rattle the bag at my side.

"Took a late one, eh?" Tommy is looking over some paperwork.

"Anyone sit there?" I ask, standing in front of the door, nodding over to the couch.

"Ah, no. We just got here. Why?" Tommy asks.

I stare at the ripped up old couch. "Some dude croaked on that couch today... Just a little while ago... It was weird."

"Whoa," Tommy's head moves back. He looks over to the couch. You can't see it real well from the attendant's station. I can tell Tommy believes me. I've never had any reason to lie or boast to him before, so why would I suddenly start now?

"Yeah? Who?" Doris jumps in, looking around, "You?"

"Not me," I gaze at the couch.

"Cool," Doris nods her head, looking from me to Tommy to the couch, "I call dibs," she perks up.

"Dibs on what?" Tommy squints.

"On crashin' on that couch tonight. ...The death couch," Doris mouths, as if bestowing it with an important imprint to set it apart from any other seating surfaces in the region. "Maybe we can charge people who want to crash on it—'sleep on the death couch, take your chances, tempt fate, cheat death.' Something like that," she exhales.

"Don't let anyone sit on it for a while," I swallow, "Probably not even cold yet."

"Yeah, maybe you can still feel the heat off the guy's body," Tommy estimates.

"It's got the fog of death about it," Doris smiles, "In fact that entire area of the building."

Eventually I make my way back to the counter, to finally eat and cash out for the night, leaving the store to the night people. I think it odd, that someone would do that, just come in, flop down, pass on to their favorite record, maybe one that reminds him of better days, of the good times of his youth, a time of no responsibilities, few pressures but playing pool and foosball and sneaking beer in the cool of a friend's basement in the summer while listening to some hard rock, as if channeling the truth itself.

The next night Doris and Tommy ask if I'd heard any more about the guy. I say no, as I hadn't. We check the obituaries and there isn't a word about the guy. We check for days on end after that too, and still find nothing. In fact, we become so curious about the guy, about who he was and what his life was about, that we decide to look into the matter. We decide to make it a project, to find out what his life was like, what happened that he'd keel over in a dingy used record store—a dilapidated one-story brick building on the unfashionable side of town—in the middle of a weekday.

So that becomes my next writing project for the journal—a running piece on that dude who was called home to the sounds of one of his favorite records, to thoughts of the glory of his youth, long summer days with nothing to do, some girl in that summer, some heavy sounds. And in thinking again about my own demise, I don't know when or where, or how it'll all go down, but man, now that's how I'd like to cash out—with some style, on an old couch in a creaky, musty used record store, to my favorite album, reliving some of those good times.

shiny things

The organ's hum reverberates as the round man strolls into the tavern. He weaves out of the bowling alley and around the tables to the adjoining bar, looking back over his shoulder for some reason. The bartender spots him instantly, as he is a regular on Tuesday and Friday nights. The round man drops in occasionally at other times too, to roll a practice ball or two, shoot a fast game of pool, grab a quick beer, but mostly he's a regular on league nights

"What'll it be?" the bartender calls, wringing a towel in a glass.

"Same," the round man responds as he reaches the bar, still looking back into the bowling alley.

Glossy black and white photos in thin black frames scatter on the wall behind the bar, above the glass shelves lined tightly with shining glasses. A car pulls into the parking lot, its lights circle the walls and catch the glass in each picture frame. They shine for just a moment.

The round man puts his foot on the rail and leans against the bar. The organ continues to float a subtle hymn as he raises a golden glass of beer—dim, golden light, golden wood all around, golden wheat stretching out for miles.

Some of the photos are of old ball players—Joe Adcock, Orlando Cepeda, Ron Santo, Mickey Mantle—guys like that. Some are of Chet Baker and Jack Kerouac types.

The organ player was a hippie at one time. He's been playing in that corner for years—ever since the early 70s, as if he'd missed out on the prime of the 60s and his playing could somehow restore it all, pull it all back. Ever since it was a cool hangout, a little hideaway which drew other hippies from hundreds of miles away. Now it's just an ordinary old bar in an ordinary old bowling alley lying in the tall weeds at the edge of town. Yet people still drop by from time to time, sometimes bringing their children to see the old hangout and the hippie, to see the place they'd heard about, the place they'd dreamt of escaping to while stuck in the middle of lonely, dull summers long ago.

Framed photos of older hippie bands circle the organ player like tattered, watchful angels—piano players like Ray Charles and old organ bands like Iron Butterfly, Spirit, Uriah Heep, Love, and Vanilla Fudge, bands with gently howling organs, whining with loneliness, stirring with emptiness. From the corner the hippie sways with his sunglasses on and eyes closed, back and forth, forward and back, from side to side with his music slowly billowing, weaving in smoky strings, circling to flower in the air.

There's a lady who watches the round man. She always watches him carefully, making sure he doesn't catch her. She slowly follows him in from the bowling alley and watches him from a safe distance. She watches him because she loves him.

The round man continues to sip his drink.

The lady leans against the back wall, blending right into it, then she steps up to a table and sits. She doesn't know what to do with her hands. She hides them in her lap. They seem to roll and flip-flop over one another, trying to get comfortable.

He has noticed her around, she knows that. She sees him around the place, in its dream-like qualities as he stands alone, off to the side of everything. Is he a loner? No one seems to talk to him. He stands alone and drinks alone. He eats alone and often bowls alone.

She wants to approach him, but he is never quite so alone. Someone else always seems to be around, seems to be too near, so she waits for him.

There is a lull between games and she hopes he sees her, hopes he'll come over and introduce himself. She sits at a table in the bar, slowly eating peanuts and watching the TV that hangs in the corner.

She longs for the day when she can approach him. She thinks about giving a letter to him, dreaming he is a thoughtful, understanding man and would not greet the situation with unkindness if she handed it to him. She has carried the worn letter in her jacket for weeks—for patient, waning, fraying and fading weeks, just in case she'd bump into him and can only stammer out a quiet hello. He might not hear her in the action of the bowling alley, and a letter doesn't speak in such a hush.

Up in the corner the TV flickers an old drama:

"I'm leaving in two days," a woman says calmly, like she is talking to herself, her voice quivering with tears. "We haven't had a chance to say good-bye. You haven't said anything to me all week. I'm leaving in two days," she is talking faster now. "I'm leaving in two days," she sighs. "I'm not sure I want to leave like this."

"You've been drinking," a man beams as a crowd roars behind the door in the hall.

"We've known each other a long time," she steps to him.

"Yeah, we've had a lot of good times," he coughs as she steps closer.

She drops her drink, throws her arms around him as it crashes on the wood floor. "Let's go," she sighs, "let's get out of here."

He grins and looks around and reaches for the doorknob in her embrace. "We just got here," he says, trying to balance his drink in her grip.

"I know, I know," she buries her head into his arm, leading him away from the door. "I know but I want to be with you," she stumbles. "I just want to be with you," she holds her head on his shoulder. She looks up and kisses him. "I've wanted to do that for, like, ever."

"We're here together," his hand circles her back. He is looking through the crack in the door, watching the churning stream of people passing in the hall.

"I want to be alone with you..." she looks up and whispers.

"OK, OK," he smiles, his voice a quiet hum.

"...All alone," she whispers, pushing him to the back of the kitchen, still embracing him. She squeezes tightly, moving him to the back door. "Hold me," she says, "...Don't let me go."

The television remote was sitting before her on the table, right in front of an empty ashtray. She reaches ahead and touches the channel button and the channel jumps forward. A couple is standing together in a phone booth in the dark of night, flakes of snow falling all around them outside.

"I didn't think you really liked me..." the lady in the phone booth says to the man standing with her. She is looking down at her shoes. "...that you were just asking me out because you ask everyone out."

"I don't know if that's the meanest thing anyone's ever said to me, or the most adorable," he says. Then he shrugs, "I haven't asked anyone out in a year or two."

She looks away, looking around for him, but he has finished paying for his beer and is walking back into the other room. She catches herself watching him and quickly turns away. Then she feels maybe she turned away too quickly and that maybe he saw, so she jumps up as if she just remembered something important and walks out as he disappears back into the bowling alley.

Balls roll down the lanes with heavy sounds of thunder, sounds of invisible momentum, some things so near, some so far, some so real, some just in the air. Crashing of pins, build-ups and releases, important things, things that are real and things that we think are real, things that we want, things that can crash all around.

She settles back into her plastic seat. Incidentally, she is a very good bowler. She's happy about that, like they have something in common, like they have something to share.

Her teammates' children are fighting in the seats next to her, squirming and hitting each other. She sits looking down into her hands in her lap. She holds them together, as if she were trying to hold him there.

Maybe, she thinks, maybe someday we'll go bowling together—and all my friends will see us here together. Maybe, someday.

About the Author

Tony Rauch is an Architect living in Minneapolis, Minnesota, USA.
In his spare time he cleans and tries to get his dog to stop barking.
On rare occasions he might write a short story.
This is his fourth arty short story collection.
For story samples, visit him online at: www. trauch.wordpress.com
Otherwise you should probably be listening to some choice rock-'n'-roll music.

– what if i got down on my knees? –

Romantic misadventures and entanglements of absurd, whimsical, existential longing, discovery, secrets, identity, escape, strange happenings, endurance, regret, and hope that serve as little postcards from the lonely regions of the human heart.

These tales of wonder are about people trying to find meaning and a place in an indifferent world, and their discoveries, revelations, secrets, failures, struggles, connections, and odd encounters along the way—

—two unemployed men steal dogs and run them through buildings around town.
—a man goes on what turns into the worst date in recorded history.
—you are asked to baby-sit for a neighbor, only to find a giant baby waiting for you.
—a man comes home to find his entire yard and home paved over by a long lost rival.
—a clerk at a used record store finds a man has passed away on one of the couches.
—some young adults go into the basement to get sad, in order to impress girls.
—a stranger extracts a baby from a man waiting for the bus.

With themes of longing, fragility, uncertainty, impermanence, regret, the mysteries hidden in everyday life, discovery, ennui, loneliness, irresponsible behavior, confusion, change, identity, and absurd situations, Tony Rauch is a worthy successor to the artistry and absurdism of Donald Barthelme and Steve Martin.